D1050567

The Story of Me

The Story of Me

Advocate

Writers Club Press
San Jose New York Lincoln Shanghai

The Story of Me

All Rights Reserved © 2000 by Advocate

No part of this book may be reproduced or transmitted
in any form or by any means, graphic, electronic, or mechanical,
including photocopying, recording, taping, or by any information
storage retrieval system, without the permission
in writing from the publisher.

Writers Club Press
an imprint of iUniverse.com, Inc.

For information address:
iUniverse.com, Inc.
620 North 48th Street, Suite 201
Lincoln, NE 68504-3467
www.iuniverse.com

This is a work of fiction and references to real people, products, and/or
organizations are included only to lend a sense of authenticity. All of the
characters, whether central or peripheral, are wholly the product of the
author's imagination, as are their actions, motivations, thoughts and
conversations, and neither the characters nor the situations which were
invented for them are intended to depict real people or real events.

ISBN: 0-595-13744-X

Printed in the United States of America

DEDICATION

This story is dedicated to my husband, Bob. His love, encouragement, companionship, and patience teaches me everyday that a soulmate isn't someone who completes you…it's someone who gives you the tools to complete yourself.

I love you.

ACKNOWLEDGEMENTS

Several people generously lent me their time and talent as beta readers and/or editors. Without them, well, let's just say I'd still be trying to figure out where to put the commas. These guys (Barbara Davies, kd bard, Ellie, Medora MacD, and Maggie Sheridan) simply rock. Any semi-colons, or other funky punctuation, were kindly supplied by them.

A special thank you goes to Medora MacD and Maggie Sheridan for their assistance with the book cover description.

Finally, I would be remiss if I didn't mention my loving spouse one more time. Thank you doesn't begin to cut it.

CONTENTS

PART I

CHAPTER *1*

"This is—because I've just discovered that I *really* suck at thinking up snappy titles—The Story of Me. And I, for the first time in my *previously* contented life, find myself in the role of storyteller. Well...there was that one time I tried to tell my sister Paula's kids a bedtime story about Godzilla and it scared them so badly they peed the bed for weeks. But that's beside the point."

An irritated dark eyebrow edged its way upward.

"Don't roll your eyes at me, you bushy-tailed rat. What *is* the point? I don't have one yet. If I have to deal with that, so do you."

The woman shifted on the cold wooden bench and tossed a few more sunflower seeds to her mostly attentive audience. The rotund squirrel leaned back on his haunches and turned to face her as he furiously nibbled his delicious treat, all the while doing his best to look terribly interested in her story. After all, the bag of seeds next to the tall, dark-haired woman was nearly full, and it wouldn't be dark for another couple of hours.

"Who am I?" she continued, undaunted, even as the first few raindrops splashed into the shallow, muddy puddles around the bench. "In addition to simply calling me the ridiculous dumbass who got roped into the biggest mess of her life over a worthless piece of tin, revenge, and a petite blonde, you can call me Randi. No, it's not short for anything. It's just Randi. Ask my parents why."

Pale blue eyes fell from the squirrel and surveyed the wet, leaf-strewn surface around her feet. With one hand she absently pulled together the lapels of her jacket as a gust of wind picked up her hair, then resettled it wildly around her shoulders. The wind and the soft, uneven pitter-patter of the rain nearly drowned out her steady but quiet voice.

"The reason I'm sitting here telling you a story on this incredibly dreary fall day, is that *she* lives in one of those apartments over there." Randi pointed to a smallish building that lined the very corner of the park. "And I'm afraid to go up and see her. That's right, afraid. Scared shitless. So I'm killing time, pure and simple. Oh God," she moaned, as if suddenly realizing she was actually talking to a beady-eyed rodent. "I just know I'm insane." Then she simply shrugged and refocused on her tale. "Are you confused yet, squirrel?" Randi nodded. "I thought so. You're not alone."

A few more seeds fell between the soggy brown leaves at the squirrel's feet.

"I promise you that I was minding my own business when *she* knocked at my door and my life got flushed down the crapper...Wait. It started a little before that, only I didn't know it at the time. I was grocery shopping at Piggly Wiggly on 11th and Broadway..."

*   *   *

It was midnight; the only time Randi could bear to go to the grocery store. She'd do almost anything to avoid the crowds and the snotty-nosed little monsters that cried when their mothers bought Shredded Wheat instead of Fruity Pebbles. The aisles were mostly empty except for a few frazzled college students, off-duty nurses and cops. Who else shops at midnight?

Randi stopped in front of the shampoo display, then turned her head to the left and right. She was alone in the aisle but someone was watching her, she was certain. When her body spoke to her, Randi listened. And it was yelling, in an unnecessarily spooky sort of voice, that she was being spied on. The hairs on the back of her neck stood at attention as the skin around them got all itchy and tingly. She wondered briefly if she should switch to dandruff shampoo.

Then she heard it…again. A squeaky shopping-cart wheel gave away her watcher's position at the end of aisle, just out of sight. Randi smiled to herself. He must have gotten one of those carts where one of the wheels is completely frozen or spins in a circle a millimeter off the ground. *Unlucky bastard!* she mused, shaking her head knowingly. For a second she felt an uncharacteristic surge of pity for her observer.

Randi wasn't surprised by the unwanted attention. She was an exceptionally attractive woman who stood out in a crowd. At 5'11" tall, the raven-haired driving instructor stood out almost everywhere. This wouldn't be the first time some guy tried to get his jollies at her expense. "He'd just better not come too close," she growled, more annoyed than frightened.

Shopping completed, she moved to the register and was disgusted to find a line of waiting customers. The young cashier was excitedly talking to the teenage boy at the head of the line whose groceries sat motionless on the conveyor belt. Randi rolled her eyes. She was going to be here a while. She could just tell.

Another customer piled in behind her, and her patience snapped. She felt trapped by the carts and people and resigned herself to try 5:00 a.m. the next time. "Hey, freak girl! You wanna hurry it up?" Randi called out to the muted cheers and laughter of the other shoppers.

The pierced, tattooed, and shockingly-dyed cashier threw Randi a lewd gesture but began moving something other than her black, lipstick-lined mouth.

Bored, Randi decided to investigate the contents of the other shoppers' arms and carts, and try to figure things out about their lives. Boredom was something the woman could simply not abide.

Two people in front of her, stood a man wearing sweat pants and a wrinkled T-shirt. He was clutching a gallon of Rocky Road ice cream and an industrial-sized bottle of pain relievers. He looked as though he had just crawled out of bed before walking into the store. He was no challenge at all; a blind man could pick out an expectant father.

Behind him stood a shaggy-looking young man whose baggy pants barely spared the other shoppers a revolting view. His glazed eyes stared at the candy bar rack with undisguised need. Then he simply dumped an entire case of Hershey Bars into his basket, crushing one of his 6 bags of Cheetos.

Randi smirked. *'Just say no,' my ass.*

The woman behind her, facing away from Randi, was plainly dressed and intently reading a copy of the National Enquirer. In her left hand she was carrying a carton of orange juice.

Randi peered over her shoulder and read the story headline. "Alien Princess has JFK's Baby." *Who can read this shit?* she wondered, even as she was trying to read the words herself. Randi never got a good look at the woman but based on her reading selection, she was content to simply think of her as a moron and move on.

Forty-three dollars later, Randi was loading 2 full bags into the back seat of her car. Suddenly, she straightened, her eyes darting around the nearly empty parking lot. She heard something…or more likely someone. "Who's there?" she called out. The lot was very dark, and Randi couldn't see into the long shadows that surrounded her. She shut her car door abruptly, mentally daring her watcher to show themselves. "Chickenshit!" she yelled, before driving home.

*   *   *

Randi leaned forward and put her elbows on her knees. "Then weird shit started happening on a daily basis. I couldn't get a good night's sleep. Someone was following me to and from everyplace I went. But I could never see them." Challenging eyes glared at the squirrel. "I was NOT just being paranoid! Ohhh…and they were good too, no doubt about that. This wasn't just one of my toked-out students out for revenge. No. Someone was putting in some serious effort."

"I started growing restless at work." Randi popped several seeds in her mouth, spitting the shells into her hand and tossing them alongside the bench. "Something was about to happen. I could literally *feel* it. Now, before you go calling me a modern day witch, let me explain. It's not like I used a crystal ball or anything. And it wasn't like these were feelings I'd never had before. What I felt was regular, run of the mill, highly intense anticipation. The problem was, I didn't know what I was anticipating. On the days when I didn't have out-and-out stomach cramps, I was nauseous all the time. I was left with this achy, unsettled feeling. But then…" Randi stopped mid-sentence and tugged a waving strand of hair behind her ear.

An elderly couple, walking arm in arm, strolled down the trail in front of Randi's bench. The low burr of their voices and the crunching of the wood chips beneath their feet interrupted her tale. When she was certain they couldn't hear what she was saying she continued speaking, happy that her squirrel friend wasn't chased away by their presence.

"But then, all that changed the night *she* showed up at my apartment."

＊　　＊　　＊

Randi was stretched out on her sofa, quite naked and completely bored…again. There were a lot of things a healthy 32-year-old woman could do while buck-naked. Randi was just tired of doing them alone.

She flipped on the television, clicking from station to station, until she was left with only a choice between 'Bay Watch' and ritual suicide. She was torn.

But at least she wasn't nauseous. She felt surprisingly good that evening and considered calling a friend to go out for a late drink. Maybe she'd meet someone while she was out? Maybe this was her body's way of telling her that she needed companionship? But that would mean leaving the apartment, and she couldn't face the knowledge that she would be followed.

It wasn't that she was afraid of her watcher. For some reason, Randi couldn't work up a respectful fear. Instead, she was irritated that she could never see him. It was like trying to remember the lyrics to a classic song but never quite getting it right. She hated to admit it, but it was making her nuts. The thought of her watcher brought back Randi's nausea, and she vowed that when she finally found out who was doing this…she'd rip him a new…

KNOCK. KNOCK. KNOCK.

Pale eyes glanced at her watch. "Who knocks on someone's door at 11:00 p.m.?" she called out loudly as she approached her front door. Not caring who it was or that she was stark naked, Randi jerked the door wide open.

"What do you want?" the driving instructor snarled, still angry with herself for choosing 'Bay Watch'.

"I…um…I want…well…" Standing in Randi's doorway was a wide-eyed blonde who looked irritatingly familiar.

Expressive eyes narrowed dangerously. "I know you, don't I?" Randi asked, uncertainty threading her voice. Was this what she had been expecting?

Nah…

The woman in the doorway shifted from one foot to the other, wondering if she'd have the nerve to follow through with her plan and feeling oddly overdressed in blue jeans and a navy rugby shirt. But she couldn't run away now. This was the moment she'd been waiting for. The moment she'd planned and agonized over for weeks. Okay, for 12 long days. She would just have to focus on her mission. *The mission is the important thing,* she told herself as she forced away her decidedly naughty thoughts centering on the gorgeous naked body before her, a pint of whipped cream and a spatula. She commanded green eyes to drift up from the full breasts that were staring her in the face to meet angry blue.

Randi's jaw went slack. "I do know you! You're that incredibly stupid woman from my driving class!" Tact had packed its bag and left town with Randi's good night's sleep days earlier.

"I am not stupid!"

"You're sure as hell not smart."

"How can you say that? You don't even know me!"

"You failed my course." Randi always remembered the people who failed her class.

"But…"

"Twice."

The blonde stomped her foot angrily. This wasn't going as she'd expected. "I missed the final exams. I was…distracted." Not feeling that she'd sufficiently made her point she added, "Just so you know, your course wouldn't challenge a monkey."

Randi considered taunting the woman by making monkey sounds but decided it would be too hard to maintain her dignity while making monkey sounds naked. She let a wickedly arched eyebrow speak for itself. "What's your name again?" She bit off the word 'blondie'. "And why are you at my front door so late?"

Ignoring the question, the shorter woman continued, still stinging from the slight on her intelligence. "Do you always answer the door naked?"

Randi's eyes narrowed, and her face began to turn an angry shade of red as realization dawned. "You're the woman from the supermarket, aren't you? That night...you were...you were reading about the alien baby!" The last part wasn't a question. The pieces were starting to fit together for Randi.

Fair eyebrows shot skyward as mental alarm bells rang. Trying not to appear as out of sorts as she felt, the woman extended her hand. "I'm Mac."

Randi remembered the woman's name now. She even had the exact same thought she'd had the first time she'd heard it. 'Mac' was such a stupid name for the short woman. Mac implied something "big". Like a Mack Truck or hell...a Big Mac! It implied a manly owner. And while the younger woman was athletic looking she was, by no means, masculine.

"I remember your name now, *Mackenzie*," Randi intoned, making it clear that she knew the younger woman did not like to be called that, but that she was going to do it anyway. Then she gasped as the last piece fell into place. "OH MY GOD!!! YOU'RE MY STALKER!"

Mac winced. 'Stalker' was such an ugly word. It was true of course, but she still didn't like being called that. "I prefer to be called Mac," she stated quietly. Mac wrung her hands together in frustration, wondering how someone only a few years her senior could make her feel like she was being scolded by her first grade teacher. *So what if I liked to eat paste? All the kids were doing it!*

A sound from behind her caused Mac to turn around. Randi's neighbor took a step out of his doorway, trash bag in hand, before he looked up and saw Randi's nude body. He froze, wide-eyed and open-mouthed.

Mac turned back to Randi, hands on hips. "Do you see what effect that has on people? Look!" She pointed over her shoulder at the man who was afraid to even blink. Drool was beginning to pool at the corners of his mouth.

Randi shot her neighbor a disgusted look and pulled her former student into her apartment. Randi's door slammed loudly as she pushed Mac against its cool surface. "Why have you been following me?! Everywhere! You've been following me everywhere!"

"That's not true," Mac replied forcefully. "It's only been a few days. And not everywhere, just where I could. I...I had to be sure..." *What did I have to be sure about again? Oh yeah,* "...that your lifestyle would work."

Randi backed away a step. Her hands were shaking. She hadn't been so close to committing an act of pure violence in years. She wanted to strangle her tormentor. Didn't the woman realize how creepy it was knowing someone was watching you and *never* being able to figure out who? Randi instantly reached out and grabbed Mac's wrist; practically dragging the smaller woman across the carpet, she flung her onto the sofa.

Mac's temper was beginning to flare. She knew she deserved a little abuse. After all, she had been, she cringed, *stalking* Randi for the past 12 days. But this was going too far. Before she could open her mouth to protest Randi's treatment, the taller woman spoke.

"Stay right where you are," Randy commanded. "I'm still deciding whether to kill you myself or just call the police and let them handle you."

"Police?" Mac's face paled.

"What did you think? That I'd be happy or flattered that some crazy woman was following me? Although, I must admit that I'm surprised it wasn't a man." Randi took a few steps backwards and removed a short robe from her hall closet.

Mac's eyes easily telegraphed relief at the gesture. Now if she could only convince Randi to play along, she would have her satisfaction. Her face creased into a frown as Randi approached her again. This wasn't going to be easy. She hadn't planned on Randi being aware that she was being followed.

Randi sat down on the coffee table facing the sofa. Piercing blue eyes bored into Mac. "What did you mean you had to make sure my lifestyle would work?" As angry as she was, Randi was still more curious.

Mac swallowed hard. She had wanted to check out how Randi lived, and whether she was married with five kids, but that was only partially true. Once she began following Randi, she couldn't seem to stop. The woman was utterly fascinating, although she seemed not to know it. Mac had used this time to build up the nerve to approach Randi. She should have done it days ago but every time she tried, something would happen, and she'd change her mind.

Gathering her courage, Mac sat up straight and laid her cards on the table. "I have a proposition for you."

Randi snorted. "I figured it was something like that. Sorry to disappoint, but anything *you* could propose wouldn't interest me. I don't 'switch hit', if you know what I mean."

Mac wasn't surprised, although she hadn't seen Randi with any men for the past 12 days either. It would have made things easier, but still…"That doesn't matter. You only have to *look* as though you do."

"What?"

"I want you to pretend to be my girlfriend."

Twin eyebrows raised. "Your girlfriend? Didn't you hear what I just said?" Randi let out an annoyed breath, more certain than ever that her original characterization of the woman's mental capacity was right on target. "Let me spell it out for you. I am *not* gay."

Mac stood up and ran an impatient hand through her short blonde hair. "I don't care whether you're *actually* gay. I just want you to *pretend* to be my girlfriend."

"Why in the hell would I do that?" Randi interrupted. "If you want a girlfriend, why not go out and get a real one? It's not like you're unattractive or anything."

* * *

"Let me interrupt here by saying *that* was a huge understatement. Even then, I knew that. Mac is not just average looking. She's beautiful in a fresh, all-American sort of way, and is pretty much the opposite of me, as far as looks go. She's only about 5'4" and has that tousled, short blonde thing going. Well, I guess reddish-blonde would be more precise. The sun does really great things with her highlights. She's trim and just a little muscular from about a gazillion hours of aerobics and weights. Christ, I thought I was a fanatic! The woman acts like missing one day is gonna kill her. Her eyes are sort of this blue-green kind of color, and I swear they change from one to the other, depending on her mood and what she's wearing."

Randi stopped and laughed at herself as the squirrel cocked his head to the side. She took in a deep breath of the fragrant moist air. "I know what you're thinking." She slowly shook her head as unexpected tears stung her eyes. "Shit," she muttered and tossed out another seed.

*   *   *

Mac just stared at Randi. "Well…um…thanks, I think." She moved back to the couch and sat down in front of the taller woman who appeared much calmer. "I'm not explaining this very well, so I'm going to lay it on the line. My family is having a 4-day get together at the end of the month. I want you to come 'as my girlfriend' and, if everything works out, we'll both get something we want."

Randi opened her mouth to speak, but Mac raised a hand to forestall her. "About 3 months ago, during the time I was in your class, my girlfriend dumped me." Mac's eyes went cold. "I guess it would be more accurate to say she *used* me and then dumped me."

Randi could already tell that Mac fidgeted when she was nervous or upset. A tiny bead of nervous perspiration rolled down Mac's throat and disappeared behind the heavy rugby shirt.

Mac's soft voice drew Randi's attention back to her. "I'm a nurse at Baptist Memorial. It seems my girlfriend had her eye on a certain doctor there, and she thought the best way to get to him would be through me." Mac took a deep breath, and stilled her hands, which were twitching nervously. "I want you to pretend to be my girlfriend so we can make my *former* girlfriend jealous." Mac knew that 'suffer' was a better term, but she would explain that soon enough.

"What makes you think my being with you will make her jealous?" Randi eyed Mac speculatively. There was something she hadn't said. "Not to belabor the point, but if she dumped you, why would she care who you're dating?"

Mac's lips curled into what could only be described as an evil grin. "Because…" she drew out the anticipation, "…my former girlfriend's name is Sandra Flax."

*   *   *

"Have you ever had one of those moments when the world around you comes to a crashing halt? When your heart beats so loudly that it drowns out every other sound? When the universe collapses to a single, solitary, radiant point of energy? This was one of those moments for me."

"The last time I heard the name Sandra Flax, Clinton was still screwing that ugly chick from Arkansas." The squirrel cocked his head to the side. "Not Hillary, the other one, before the chubby kid." The squirrel still looked confused. "Fine! It was 1989. Anyway, the sound of Sandra's name sent shivers down my spine and reawakened a hatred so venomous, at one time I thought it would be my undoing."

Another squirrel joined the one at Randi's feet and began milling around for anything her mate might have missed. Randi smiled at her antics and rewarded her with a treat of her own before continuing.

"Sandra and I were, at one time, the best of friends. In a weird sort of way we complemented each other, both emotionally and intellectually. Where I was quiet and somewhat standoffish, she was outgoing and a little wild. And we both excelled in math. Together, we decided to use our talents as a way out of small town hell."

"We entered a two-day statewide mathematics competition as a team. To be honest, I pretty much sucked at everything else in school and my grades showed it. This was my ticket to college. My *only* ticket. The winners would receive a full scholarship."

Randi's voice shook a little as she spoke. "I was sooo ready. I spent months preparing. Endless equations ran through my head, until I thought I'd go mad. But I wasn't going to be denied. My parents were against my entering the competition. They thought college was a waste of time for women anyway. When I was packing for the trip to the competition, my father came into my bedroom and simply forbade me to attend and waste *anymore* of my time. Time that could have been spent helping him on the farm."

Randi stopped talking and took a long sip of water from the bottle that sat perched against her leg. She stopped tossing down seeds and simply stared at the trees ahead of her. The squirrels looked at each other, then back at their storyteller. Was she finished? They had only begun to feast!

The tall woman sighed. "I'm getting a little long winded about this part, aren't I? Let me give you the short version. We were scheduled to compete on the first day of the competition. But instead of showing up at the auditorium, Sandra was fucking some guy in the back of his parents' shag carpeted van. She told me about the shag carpet later. We were disqualified. Sandra's new boyfriend, the person the entire state expected to win, happened to be scheduled for the second day of the competition. One teenage fuck later, he dumped his regular partner, another loser in the game of life, and guess who replaced him? Big surprise now…Sandra! They won the whole damn thing, including a little 1st place medal. The traitorous bitch wore it everyday for the rest of our senior year! And, I was locked out of the house when I tried to go home."

*   *   *

"Tell me you didn't say Sandra Flax," Randi said seriously.

"I did."

"Sandra is gay?!" Randi's face twisted in fury. "God dammit! She fucked away my future, and she's not even interested in men! Bitch!"

"Well, that's not exactly true. It seems she can't make up her mind. She dumped me for a man."

"Rotten bitch!"

"Uh huh. And to make things even worse, the man is my own brother."

"Deceitful bitch!"

"She wanted a doctor. My brother is a doctor."

"Money-grubbing bitch!"

When it came to Sandra, Randi's vocabulary was seriously limited, and Mac was starting to wonder how they could pull this off if all Randi could do was curse. But to Mac's relief, Randi at last appeared interested in her offer.

"I take it Sandra told you about me." Randi knew Sandra was as obsessed with the medal as she was.

"She did or I wouldn't be here." Mac didn't want to go into the next part. Truth be told, it made her uncomfortable. If even half of what Sandra had said was true, Randi was not a person to be trifled with. "She said you made her life a living hell trying to steal that medal and that more than once you tried to rip it off her shirt. She claims you have some ridiculous idea that it should have been yours."

Mac could see Randi's anger growing even hotter. And she fanned the flames, using Randi's hatred to her own advantage. "She told me that she enjoyed making you suffer over the medal." *Shit, that was a low blow. What am I doing?* Mac asked herself, disturbed at the lengths she herself was willing to go to for petty revenge. But she couldn't stop. Not now. It was too late to be nice. She'd already crossed the line.

"That bitch!" Randi seethed.

"She *really* hates you."

"Good."

"Will you help me?"

"So this is all about revenge, not just making Sandra jealous? Sandra's going to be at your family gathering with your brother, and you want to torture her by my mere presence? Maybe get her interested in you again, so you can turn the tables?" Randi loved the idea, and she secretly respected Mac's plan even though she was furious with the woman for stalking her. It was devious and cruel, and if Randi were a cat she would have been purring.

Mac stretched to her full height, ready to proudly confess her sins and admit her own obsession. "You're right. I don't want her back." In fact, Mac considered her 6 months with Sandra the biggest mistake of her life. There was no way in hell, under any circumstances, that she wanted Sandra back. "It will kill her to have you there. And when she sees how happy and completely in love we are, it should be the final nail in her coffin."

Randi wanted to do this. Oh, how she wanted it! But Mac was a crazy stalker, and she'd have to pretend to be in love with her. She didn't even find Brad Pitt attractive, and he was as womanly as a man could be! She didn't know if she could do it.

Mac could see her wavering on the edge, and she played her final card. "I have it," she baited.

"Have what?" Randi leaned forward until she was nearly nose-to-nose with the smaller woman. *She can't mean...*

"The medal. I have the medal. Sandra left it on our bedroom dresser when she moved out. She wants it back, but so far I've refused." Mac fought hard not to smirk. *Gotcha, Randi.* "If you help me and we're successful, I'll give it to you." She wasn't taking any chances. If Randi couldn't be convincing, she'd end up even more humiliated than before.

Randi tried not to look overly interested, but she knew she was failing miserably. She still wanted to pummel Mac, but this was a once in a lifetime opportunity. Sweet revenge! This would ROCK!!!!

"There are conditions."

"Yess!!" Mac pumped her fist in victory. This was going to be so good. It didn't hurt that Randi was gorgeous and charming. *Too bad she hates me,* Mac thought a little sadly. Composing herself, she readied herself for negotiations. "What conditions?"

"Absolutely no touching."

"What?" Mac practically screamed.

"You heard me. No touching."

"I'm trying not to be *totally* insulted by that remark, but it's pretty damn hard," Mac ground out. She'd had about all the rejection she could take. Her self-esteem didn't need another blow. "How can we be convincing if we don't touch each other? We're supposed to be in love."

Randi had to admit Mac had a good point, but she wasn't ready to concede. "Even if I were in love with you, which would be impossible, I wouldn't be all touchy. I'm not like that."

"Unacceptable. My family doesn't know you, so they'll find it odd if we aren't affectionate. If we can't even convince them, there's no way we'll convince Sandra."

Randi scratched her chin. Maybe her stalker wasn't as stupid as she had first suspected. She didn't like the idea but had to admit that if she had to touch someone, Mac wouldn't be a bad choice. She was cute in a girly sort of way. "No kissing then. I'll hold hands and give you hugs, but that's it."

Mac frowned. "Unacceptable."

"God Dammit!!" Randi exploded. Her stalker was totally unreasonable!

"I'll offer you minimal kissing, only when necessary to convince an audience. And I'll sleep on the floor."

"Like I was gonna sleep with you anyway, *Stalker*," Randi snorted.

Mac's eyes turned into slits, but she decided to let the jibe pass. She was sooo close. "My parents are very liberal. We'll be given a room together with one bed. But after everyone is asleep, I'll move to the floor so you can have a little privacy." She knew she was asking a lot, especially from a straight stranger. But this was an all or nothing type of situation.

Randi's jaw worked back and forth silently. Mac had made another good point. She could already tell that was going to happen a lot, and she didn't like it. "Fine. You sleep on the floor. But I want Sandra to see me wearing the medal on the last day." Mac opened her mouth but Randi kept right on talking. "This point is non-negotiable. I've gone 16 years without the medal and as much as I want it, every time I've tried to get it has caused me nothing but grief. If I don't get my way on this, you'll have to find another *girlfriend.*"

Mac was surprised by the rational admission from Randi. Maybe she wasn't the psycho that Sandra painted her. Mac was honest enough with herself to admit that this had the potential to explode in her face. She even knew it was petty and spiteful. But something in Mac just wouldn't sit idly by while Sandra ran roughshod over her life. The smaller woman grinned and stuck out her palm.

Blue and green eyes locked as they shook hands, united in purpose. Randi wasn't bored anymore.

CHAPTER 2

"You won't believe what I did next. I drove her home! I gave my stalker girlfriend a lift back to her apartment! She told me she was going to walk, and I refused to allow it." Randi stopped and smirked a little. "Heh. I wasn't going to start out letting her be the 'man' in this relationship, and I said as much. For some reason she didn't seem to find it as humorous as I did. Anyway…Didn't she know how dangerous it could be walking alone at night? What if some weirdo decided to follow her home? Ha!" Randi laughed, enjoying the irony even now.

Pale eyes drifted upward, gazing quietly at the dull gray sky. What had begun as an uneven trickle was now a steady but light rain. But Randi didn't care. She was already soaked to the bone and icy cold. She wondered wistfully what it would take to feel truly warm again.

"Apparently, Mac had gotten another speeding ticket earlier that day, and when the cop ran a check on her license, and found she hadn't completed her court mandated driving school, he confiscated her license on the spot. She had taken a taxi to my apartment that evening. You wouldn't know about this, being squirrels and all, but our lovely state government has decided that if you get more than one driving violation in a year you earn a not-so-free pass to driving school. Do not pass 'GO.' Do not collect $200."

"The class only lasts about 6 hours along with a final exam the next night, but people *hate* it…and me by extension." Randi shrugged as though it didn't bother her and stuffed her hand into her jacket pocket.

The female squirrel sighed knowingly, far too quiet to be heard by human ears. It was painfully obviously that it *did* bother the storyteller.

"It seems that I represent the evil, fascist State that is infringing upon its citizenry's inalienable, God-given right to drive 80 mph in a school zone." Randi let out an unhappy breath, causing a puff of fog to escape her lips and disappear into the cold autumn air.

"Mac insisted that the fact that she ended up in my class last summer, was purely coincidental. She swore that she hadn't figured out I was *that* Peterson, until she saw my full name printed on the letter, telling her she'd failed the course. And even then she wasn't totally sure."

Suddenly, Randi clapped her hands together causing both squirrels to jump a little. "Exactly! I didn't believe her at first either! But then I realized that there was really no way for students to know my first name." Randi lowered her voice as though her next statement was a secret. "My boss makes me wear this dorky nametag that says 'Ms. Peterson' on it." Blue eyes rolled in disgust. "I hate it," she grumbled, not offering her audience any further explanation. She decided the squirrels didn't need to know that the nametag was one of those large, obnoxious, yellow happy faces. How much humiliation should one woman have to bear?

"I hesitantly agreed to meet Mac for dinner later that week. We didn't have that long until 'ShowTime,' and she insisted that we needed to get to know each other if we were going to pull this off. When Mac said it, it made so much sense. She can actually be very persuasive when she wants to be. My original assessment of her was way off. She's not stupid. In fact, she's quite intelligent. Why in the hell did she ever hook up with Sandra? Of course, I guess I could ask myself that same question."

"We spent the short car ride to her apartment in quiet conversation planning our 'date'. It was so normal it was frightening. What was I doing? Did I think revenge was worth going to these ridiculous extremes? Oh yeaaaah, baaaby. I sure did."

"Mac also promised that I wouldn't see or *feel* her, until we met at the restaurant later in the week. I thought that would make my nausea go away. It didn't."

*   *   *

Randi rushed into her apartment and clicked on the light next to the television. Her last class had run a little late, and she knew she'd have to fly to make it on time. Mac had said the restaurant was casual, and Randi had already shampooed her hair that morning, going with a dandruff shampoo just in case. But she still needed to pick out something to wear and find the place. She was certain it was one of those trendy type college places she just hated.

Rummaging through the closet, she selected a soft V-neck, crimson sweater and pair of black jeans. Randi brushed her teeth and hair, deciding to wear it down in order to save time. A quick coat of lipstick and she was grabbing her black leather jacket.

On the way to the front door, the driving instructor stopped dead in her tracks and began howling with laughter. Meeting her stalker for dinner was the closest thing she'd had to a date in months! "How's that for a sad commentary on my life?" she mumbled to her Chia Pet on the way out the door.

*   *   *

Mac selected a booth at the very front of the restaurant so she could people watch. The nurse glanced at her watch as she slid across the cold vinyl seat, glad she wasn't as late as she'd thought she'd be.

The hostess deposited two menus on the table before motioning the waitress over to take Mac's drink order. The blonde ordered a bottle of light beer then leaned back heavily into the bouncy cushion to await Randi's arrival. Didn't Randi have the common courtesy not be late?

She herself had risked losing her newly regained driver's license in order to be here on time. Well, almost on time.

The nurse didn't have to wait long before she spied Randi's lanky form through the tinted glass of the restaurant's picture window. Mac chastised herself and her body's immediate response to the taller woman. But damn, the woman *was* fine! She found it hard to believe that Sandra, the slut, had ever been able to keep her hands off Randi. She made a mental note to ask Randi about that later and took another deep swallow of beer.

Mac chuckled as Randi walked right past the restaurant. A few moments later the tall woman walked past the door again, this time in the opposite direction. Mac felt no compulsion to get up and assist the darker woman. She was enjoying her beer way too much to want to move, and besides, her feet were tired and achy. She knew Randi would find her way in sooner or later. If it turned out to be later, Mac would just order another beer and wait some more. She could be very patient when the mood struck her.

Last night, thank God, was Mac's last turn at the nightshift. She'd finally built up enough seniority to get a permanent dayshift, and her bloodshot eyes were eternally grateful. While the hellish shift made watching Randi possible, it was plainly killing the younger woman. Mac briefly wondered how much sleep deprivation and her recent, but highly detailed, driving instructor/student fantasy—this one involved using the seatbelts in a way that would give JD Powers and Associates a collective woody well into the new millennium—had to do with her current plan.

On her third pass by the restaurant, Randi caught Mac's smiling face through the glass. The driving instructor looked up and finally noticed the restaurant's banner, which was partially obscured by a low hanging tree branch. She cursed vehemently as she watched Mac mouth the words "oh shit," then try to hide her face behind her tall menu.

Randi marched proudly through the front door and straight over to Mac. "Hello, *Stalker!*" she sneered loud enough for the other patrons to turn their heads. Randi punctuated her greeting with a slap on the back that was a little too firm to be entirely friendly. Mac began furiously choking on her beer as Randi walked around the table and slid into her half of the booth looking supremely annoyed.

"What did you call me?" Mac finally hissed in a low voice as she tried to push back her impending blush. People were staring.

"You heard me, *Stalker,*" Randi hissed back in an equally distasteful tone.

Each woman childishly decided to ignore the other. They focused solely on their menus for several long moments until Randi couldn't take it anymore. For some unknown reason, Mac didn't appear at all affected by this little game. Damn, but that woman *was* patient when she wanted to be! "Mackenzie," Randi muttered in a more conciliatory voice.

Mac ignored Randi for a few more satisfying seconds before lowering her menu just enough for dancing green eyes to appear over the top. She smiled sweetly. "Yes? And please call me Mac."

Blue eyes glinted with anger—or maybe it was frustration. Randi wasn't sure. But the instructor could see that Mac was completely unrepentant. "Tonight was *your* idea so you'd better make it count, because it won't be happening again…*Stalker,*" she added in a voice every bit as sugary as Mac's, just to piss her off.

Mac knew she'd pushed the older woman too far. But there was something about Randi that sparked an evil streak in her. This type of childish behavior was so *not* Mac. But she just couldn't help herself. It was like Randi was challenging her very existence with each look.

Mac was already beginning to despise that overly used dark eyebrow, even though she did find it sexy in an annoying sort of way. Just like Randi. Mac sighed. She wanted to be nicer to the woman. She really did.

"I'm sorry, Randi. I really do want this to work." Mac reached across the table and laid her hand on Randi's forearm. "Let's start ov…"

Randi jerked her arm away violently. "What do you think you're doing?" she asked angrily.

Mac looked stunned, then hurt. Why was Randi's reaction so violent? She was trying to apologize! "I…I…I'm sorry. I didn't mean to startle you. I…"

*　　*　　*

"Don't look at me that way. Just don't! I know it was a cold-hearted thing to do. But I truly didn't mean to react that way. She just surprised me, and a big part of me was still angry that she let me walk around outside the restaurant like an idiot. I felt like she was laughing at me. And I really meant it when I told her I wasn't a touchy person."

Randi shifted slightly and kicked a pebble away from the toe of her boot. "She got all sad-looking, and those soft, green eyes turned watery. When she brought her eyes back up to meet mine, I felt like someone was ripping my guts out. Why?" Randi slowly shook her head. "I still have no idea. But I decided then and there that I couldn't stand to see her hurt…ever." Randi smiled wryly. "Of course, that didn't keep us from mixing like oil and water. It just made me aware that when she was truly miserable, I would be too. Just my luck, huh? I was somehow 'in tune' with my very own, most likely insane, most definitely irritating, *stalker girlfriend*. Oh boy…"

*　　*　　*

Mac stood up and threw her napkin in Randi's face. "Forget it! Forget the whole damn thing!" With tears in her eyes, she turned to leave, but her feet stopped of their own accord when she heard Randi calling after her.

"Wait!" Randi slid out of the booth and moved in front of Mac. "Can we sit back down?" Blue eyes scanned the restaurant, and Mac followed their gaze. Every head in the place was turned in their direction. "Please," she said as nicely as she could. When Mac looked unmoved she added, "I'm sorry." The driving instructor was even successful in not rolling her eyes…mostly. Not only was her stalker unreasonable, but she was touchy too!

Mac eyed Randi warily, carefully trying to gauge whether the taller woman was sincere. "All right," she said a little hesitantly, as she moved back toward their table.

Randi expelled a relieved breath. How was she going to get her revenge, and that medal, if she kept antagonizing Mac? It was obvious that the woman was the sensitive, high-maintenance type. *Ha! Serves you right, you bitch, Sandra!*

"Since you've been stalk…err…since you already know more about me than I know about you, why don't you tell me about yourself?"

Mac smiled and launched into nothing short of a dissertation. She continued through the meal and into the dessert before taking a break.

Randi found herself enjoying the sound of the younger woman's voice as well as the pasta and wine. She was on her fourth glass when Mac finally stopped her nervous chatter.

Mac set down her cup of coffee and stared worriedly at Randi. "Do you always drink this much?" Her brow creased. She couldn't remember any trips to the liquor store.

"Do you always talk this much?"

"Yes."

"Then I'll always drink this much."

"Hardy Har…"

RING RING. RING RING.

"Excuse me."

Randi's eyes widened. Why the hell did Mac need a cell phone? Why did anyone need a cell phone? Were nurses on call like doctors? For a moment Randi was envious. Mac had talked a lot about her job, no…her career. She clearly loved it. Randi wasn't so lucky.

As Mac spoke quietly into the phone, Randi began to replay what had turned into a fairly pleasant evening. Did Mac expect Randi to remember everything about her, from her childhood pet—not that she could forget a turtle named Fru Fru—to the brand of her perfume? Randi frowned, knowing she'd be able to remember. *Who cares what her perfume is called? She smells fantastic.* Randi shook her head fiercely. *NO! I did not just think that!*

"What?" Mac began shouting into the tiny phone. "You can't do that!"

Randi leaned back and debated the merits of another glass of Merlot. She decided against it. If she was thinking about how Mac smelled, then she'd already had one too many. Her attention drifted to Mac's eyes as they changed from sea-green to a more avocado color. *Someone's in deep shit…and it's not me,* she said to herself in a sing song voice.

"But…But…" Mac's face turned red.

Randi began counting down from ten, ready to duck for cover when the younger woman simply exploded.

"You can't just expect…Yes, I know…But…That's impossible! They can't all be…" Mac rolled her eyes and gritted her teeth. Didn't anyone respect planning? "Okay. Fine. Yes, I love you, too."

Now *that* got Randi's attention. The driving instructor leaned forward and pretended to be rifling through the sugar packets on the table as she eavesdropped. She wondered whether her *girlfriend* was cheating on her already. The nerve! Randi had a certain social reputation to maintain! Of course, now it would be as a lesbian…but still…

"I'll see you then, daddy. Goodbye." Mac clicked the phone shut so violently the cover fell off into her ice cream sundae. Pushing the bowl away in disgust, Mac laid her palms flat on the table in a visible effort to calm herself. She closed her eyes briefly, and when she reopened them, her gaze shot right through Randi.

The older woman swallowed hastily. This was bad. This was so bad. She could just tell. "Wh…what's wrong?"

"Our plans have changed." Mac narrowed her eyes as her face took on a determined expression. Sandra wasn't going to get off the hook no matter what hell she had to endure!

Randi's stomach sank. "What do you mean changed?"

"My family gathering has been rescheduled from the end of the month to this Friday."

Randi blew out a relieved breath. "Is that all? Jesus, you had me worried for a minute. It'll be a pain having to get someone to cover my classes on Friday and Monday but…"

Mac braced herself. She did not want to tell Randi this part. "The gathering is in Las Vegas."

"What?!" Randi roared. "Las Vegas is at least 1500 miles away!" Her nostrils flared. "Just when were you going to let me in on this tiny bit of information, you manipulative little…"

Mac looked up from her coffee cup and winced, knowing she truly deserved Randi's wrath. Why was she always making idiotic decisions when it came to Randi? "I was going to tell you tonight," she said quietly. "I was afraid to mention it before, because I thought you might not agree to the plan." Mac fiddled with her cup. "And I *really* wanted you to say yes." The blonde didn't even want to *think* of all the reasons why that was true.

"Shit! Do you know how much airline tickets are going to cost with only three days notice? How much money do you think driving instructors make?"

Oh God. Randi was going to really freak out now. Mac just knew it. The smaller woman pulled over what was left of the bottle of wine; filling her glass to the brim, she drank it down in one long swallow. Then she shuddered. "God, this is revolting!" Randi had horrible taste in wine.

Mac set down her empty glass. "Umm…we won't have to worry about plane tickets." She shifted nervously and waited for the inevitable…Ugh! There it was. That damned arched eyebrow.

"And why is that?" Randi's voice was a deep, dangerous purr.

"Because this happens to be the week of the American Medical Association's annual meeting, in Las Vegas." She sighed wishing she could make Randi believe that this wasn't how she planned things. *If it weren't for bad luck…* "All the airline tickets have been sold out for weeks."

"What about Tucson?"

"Nope."

"Reno?"

A blonde head shook.

"Lake Tahoe?"

Mac winced again.

"Anything west of the GOD DAMNED MISSIFUCKINGSSIPPI RIVER???!" Randi boomed, causing the glasses on their table to rattle.

"No," Mac answered in a remarkably calm voice, considering the hostess was probably on her way to call the police and have her and Randi escorted out of the restaurant.

"How can you be…"

"My father checked everywhere before he called me. The only way we'll make it on time is to drive ourselves. If we leave in the morning we should make it in plenty of time."

"Are you suggesting that I spend nearly 3 days in a car alone with you, *Stalker*? Just for petty revenge?"

"Yes."

Randi shrugged. "Okay."

*　　*　　*

"You're probably wondering why I agreed so quickly to what was going to be an undoubtedly horrible trip. Simple. By that time, I had already spent days fantasizing about the look of utter horror that was sure to grace Sandra's face when she saw me. The obsession that I thought was peacefully sleeping came roaring back to life. I didn't like the person it made me, and I didn't like the things it made me do. But I was going through with it anyway. I was totally screwed."

"To add to my misery, my feelings for Mac were already starting to get confused. I wanted to lump her together with Sandra or think of her as a complete nut job. But after only one evening, I found I had more in common with my stalker than I ever would have expected."

Randi's forehead creased. "Maybe 'in common' isn't the right way to describe it. Honestly, the only thing we had in common was hating Sandra. But beyond that, there was something comfortable about Mac that I could see myself getting used to. In another life we might have been able to be good friends. I was a little sad that in this life that already seemed impossible."

Randi pulled her gloves out of her pocket and slipped them on, happy with the way her fingers warmed instantly. The rain had stopped, but the air was so heavy with moisture that she wasn't drying off. She coughed a little, then shifted her frozen ass. Park benches are not comfortable for marathon storytelling sessions.

Randi tossed out another few seeds, but the male squirrel didn't move to take them. He had grown full long ago, and now he was just along for the story. Humans were so fascinating! His mate, having joined mid-tale, enjoyed another seed then snuggled up to her partner for a bit of warmth. This was better than watching the human joggers trying to avoid the piles of dog shit!

"You're also probably wondering why anyone would go to such extremes for revenge and a tiny medal. I mean the medal probably cost all of $.89, and it wasn't even engraved. Maybe if I tell you a little more about me, you'll understand better."

"I told you that when I came home from the competition, my father had locked me out of the house? So there I was, sixteen years old, with no place to live. Now don't go pulling out your violins just yet. This isn't a movie of the week, for Christ's sake. I didn't turn to a life of crime or prostitution or anything like that. I moved in with my grandmother and finished my last year of high school. I hated life on the farm anyway. So, in a weird way, Sandra did me a favor in that regard."

"If she'd left me alone at that point, I think I would have been okay. But the bitch just couldn't. She enjoyed her victory but even more than that…she enjoyed my loss. She reveled in it and rubbed my face in it every chance she got. Which was often. The medal represented everything and nothing, the dreams of a teenager and opportunities lost. 'It was the best of times. It was the worst of times'. Heh. Just kidding." Randi smiled but it didn't quite reach her eyes. "I wanted it because she didn't want me to have it. And Sandra always seemed to get what she wanted. It was time to change that. We just had to get there first."

CHAPTER 3

"After ten more minutes of arguing over whose car we would take, I finally agreed to let Mac pick me up in hers. She insisted that because it was *her* family's gathering, at *her* parents' home, *she* should drive. I know. It made no sense to me either. Just go with it. I did." Randi set the half-full water bottle back on the bench beside her.

"I hate being driven around. It puts you at the mercy of the driver, and I was certain I didn't want to be at Mac's mercy. Of course—and this does appear to be a habit of Mac's—she left out one small detail about the trip."

*   *   *

"You drive a Volkswagen Bug?!" Randi looked as if she'd just stepped in something.

"Fahrvergnügen."

The driving instructor slid on her sunglasses and peered at Mac over the top of the cherry-red, cockroach-like vehicle. "What did you say? Far from pukin'?" Randy asked, looking back at the car. "Actually, I'm getting pretty close to it just looking at this ugly piece of crap."

"I said Fahrvergnügen; you remember, from that advertising campaign?" Mac explained through a clenched jaw. How long was this car ride again?

"Fuck Wayne Newton?" Randi wrinkled her nose and shook her head vigorously, purposely baiting the blonde.

"Smartass!"

"Well, we *are* going to Las Vegas." The older woman pulled down her sunglasses and gazed innocently at Mac. "And here I thought you were into chicks."

"Just get in, you big dumb..." Mac's sentence trailed off under her breath.

God, I love messing with her, Randi mused. Then she looked at the car again. Didn't Mac realize how unsafe these runty vehicles were? "We're taking my car."

"We are not," Mac practically snorted.

"I'll be squished! Look at me." Randi made a sweeping motion indicating the length of her body.

"If you insist." Mac smiled sexily and started at Randi's toes. Green eyes moved with exaggerated slowness, taking in every inch of Randi's lanky frame. The younger woman wasn't shy about letting her appreciation show.

"That's not what I meant." Randi didn't know whether to be angry or flattered. To her further embarrassment, she began to blush under Mac's perusal.

"I just did what you asked," Mac argued innocently. Was the taller woman actually blushing? Mac found that cute in the extreme. "Besides, you can just push the seat back for more leg room. It's too late to argue. You already agreed that we're taking my car."

Randi looked as though she would protest further, so the nurse kept pressing. "Look Randi..." Mac's hands came to rest on her hips in a gesture Randi was already beginning to recognize. "We're going to have to compromise to get through this week. Think of this compromise..." she paused, then smiled so broadly the corners of her eyes crinkled, "...as the first of *many*."

*   *   *

"When Mac was right...she was right." Randi stood up and stretched. How did people with those nerdy computer jobs stand it? Her ass was already numb and she'd only been sitting on the bench for a couple of hours.

"I think I'll simply call this next part of my story "Day 1: The Road Trip from Hell." Randi smiled proudly. "Maybe I am getting a little better at thinking up snappy titles!" The squirrels continued to stare blankly at her. "No?"

*   *   *

"What's wrong?" Mac asked slightly alarmed as she glanced over at the older woman. The blonde merged into a westbound county road and accelerated past a slower moving car. She was convinced that by using back roads, she'd save time in the long run.

Randi wiped the sleep from her eyes and tried to get comfortable. After the first 200 miles Mac's words began to blur, then, thankfully, they faded out completely. When she woke up an hour later, the younger woman was still happily chatting away. "I don't feel so good."

Mac bit her lower lip and nodded. Randi didn't look so good either. "Is there anything I can do?" She reached out to pat Randi's leg but stopped mid-motion. The nurse tried to be nonchalant as she laid her hand to rest on her own leg.

Blue eyes closed as Randi felt a pang of guilt. It was obvious that Mac was making a concentrated effort to avoid physical contact with her. It was equally obvious that doing so ran completely counter to Mac's personality. Randi sighed. She was certain there was no way in hell Mac would accept an apology for her behavior in the restaurant so decided to ignore the issue…at least for now. After all, she didn't *have* to let Mac touch her now. That wasn't part of the deal. Randi firmed her resolve, even though doing so made her feel like shit. It was her decision, and she was comfortable sticking with it. Right?

"I could drive, you know," Randi finally commented.

"You're sick, aren't you?" Mac asked worriedly. She wondered to which one of them the curse was permanently attached. She frowned. Maybe the answer was both.

"No," Randi replied stubbornly.

Mac raised an eyebrow of her own.

No one ever understood the next part although it seemed perfectly reasonable to Randi. *Fuck! I hate telling people this!* "I get car sick sometimes," she offered sheepishly.

"What?" Mac stifled a disbelieving laugh. She had to be joking.

Randi grumpily folded her arms across her chest. "What's so hard to believe about that?"

"Other than the fact that you are a *driving* instructor?"

"And did we do any actual *driving* in my class?"

Mac's brow creased. They hadn't. But still…

"Look how fast you're going!" Randi pointed to the speedometer needle that was nearly buried. She swallowed weakly. "And is it really necessary to change lanes every ten seconds?"

Randi's words were still hanging in the air when Mac noticed flashing red lights in her rear view mirror. "Damn! I *cannot* get another ticket! I'll lose my license."

The word 'again' was poised at the tip of Randi's very sarcastic tongue when, in a panic, Mac slammed on her brakes, causing Randi to jerk forward. A second later the smaller woman changed her mind and punched the accelerator.

"Ohhh, God…" Randi moaned as her stomach churned. "What…?" She turned furious eyes on Mac. "…in the hell are you trying to do?!"

Mac's mouth shaped into a tight-lipped smile. For a moment she considered trying to lose the cop. It could be done. She'd seen it on television. This wasn't Los Angeles. There wouldn't be helicopters or spotlights or dramatic chases that would later be shown on 'COPS'. She could turn off on some dirt road and just get lost for a bit. The cop would probably get bored after a few minutes and stop for donuts, or a romantically inclined sheep. Gods above, why didn't she get a turbo when she had the chance?

Randi moaned again, and Mac rolled her eyes as she reluctantly brought her 'Dukes of Hazard' fantasy to a close. Besides, she hadn't even gotten to Daisy Duke yet, and that was *always* the best part. "Fine. I can take a hint."

Mac pulled the car over onto the narrow shoulder and waited as the officer readied himself in the squad car. Randi was just trying her level best not to vomit in the front seat.

* * *

Randi sat down on the bench and shifted a bit until she was comfortable. Then she leaned forward and looked directly at the squirrels. "You're not going to believe this next bit. I still can't believe it myself."

"In the time it took for that pudgy cop to get out of his car and waddle over to the Volkswagen…"—both squirrels looked at each other and at the same time exclaimed, "Fahrvergnügen!" Randi looked a little confused by the strange sounding chirps but continued with her tale, "…Mac hatched a ridiculous plan. That woman can get into more trouble quicker than anyone I have ever met…well, anyone *except* me. You would not believe the lengths a person will go to in order to keep their driver's license."

* * *

"I've already said I'm sorry a million times. How many more times do you want me to say it?"

"Keep going and I'll let you know," Randi groused as she glared at the smaller woman, wondering whether this state had the death penalty. Did it matter? Would it stop her from killing Mac? Probably not. Randi was always an instant gratification sort of a gal.

With one hand, Mac rubbed red-rimmed eyes. What was wrong with her lately? She had to admit that making split-second decisions was never her forte. When she didn't stop and think about what she was doing, things usually turned out badly…not *this* badly, but badly nonetheless.

Could Mac's plan to utterly crush and humiliate her former girl-friend, while knocking her snotty older brother down a peg or two, have done something to upset her normally infallible good sense? She couldn't see how.

The cell door slammed shut with a hollow clank that echoed through the cavernous room. The elderly jailer fiddled with the lock for a moment before slowly walking down the short hall and out of the cellblock.

He'd placed the two women in a cell together even though the cell across from them sat empty. The way the two of them had argued bit-terly throughout the entire booking process had clued the jailer into the fact that they were a couple…that and the fact that Mac had offered to perform Randi's cavity search. The way the little blonde lit into the darker one reminded him of his dearly departed wife, Bertha, the nagging bitch…God rest her soul. So that's why he'd locked 'em up…together. The purpose of jail was to punish after all.

Randi tried not to look at Mac as she heard the beginnings of more sniffles. *She had better not be crying again!* Those crocodile tears hadn't worked with the cop the first or third time, and they weren't going to work on Randi. Was the taller woman supposed to forgive Mac any-thing just because she was all sad and weepy? Yep. Blue eyes softened as

Mac wiped her face and tried not to look as upset as she truly was. And Randi inexplicably felt her anger start to melt away.

Randi sighed. They had places to go and lives to destroy. It was time to kiss and make up. Well, maybe not kiss. Tucked in the corner of the cell was a cot that was covered with a thin, stained mattress. The cot's frame protested loudly as the taller woman sat down and crossed her long legs.

"I'd offer you a Kleenex, if I had one." Randi felt a little awkward about making the first gesture of peace. After all, this was *totally* Mac's fault. But she could be adult and mature…if she *had* to be.

"Thanks." Mac smiled a little as she moved across the cell and joined Randi on the small cot. "I'd offer you something to settle your stomach, if I had it."

Randi graced Mac with a lopsided grin that caused Mac's smile to widen further. "Thanks. But…um…I actually feel a lot better now." Especially now that Mac didn't look so dejected.

"Which do you think carries a stiffer penalty: solicitation or assault?"

Randi chewed her lip for a moment. "My assault charge…definitely."

"Mmm…" Mac was inclined to agree. She'd always heard that it was really bad to hit a cop. So it only made sense that kneeing one in the groin…twice…would get you in a lot of trouble.

"I didn't know you were just flirting to try to get out of the ticket." Randi's words came out in a rush. Seeing Mac turn all sweet and coy with that porky cop had caused a knot to form in the pit of Randi's already upset stomach. "And then when he put his hands on you like that I…I…"

Mac laid her hand on Randi's. As soon as she felt her companion's warm skin she realized what she was doing…*again*…and began to lift it off. Why was she constantly compelled to touch Randi? It was making her crazy and confused. Randi wouldn't be interested in her. Ever.

But that didn't stop her from wanting some sort of physical contact. *Any* contact.

Randi stopped Mac's withdrawal with a gentle tug on her fingers. It was okay if plotting partners occasionally touched each other, right? After all, she didn't want Mac to start crying again.

Mac leaned her head against the back wall and closed her eyes as a contented sigh escaped her lips. Randi's hand was soft and strong at the same time, and she decided instantly that she liked the feel of it in hers. "It's not your fault. I don't know *what* I was thinking."

"Apparently, you seriously underestimated the impact of your girlish charm."

"Apparently," Mac laughed, all the while wishing that Randi wasn't immune to whatever 'charm' she might possess. "That's the last time I bat my eyes at someone named Bubba. I swear, I never thought he'd actually grope me!" Her smile turned wry. "I was gearing up to clock the guy myself. You just beat me to the punch, that's all."

Randi nodded. She'd seen Mac draw her fist back as she was retching into the ditch alongside the road. And when she saw the cop's hands on Mac's boobs, she'd just lost it. Period. That bastard totally fabricated the solicitation charge after Mac rejected his blunt advances. God, where was a good mouthpiece when you needed one? She'd love to sue the crap out of this entire shit for brains county.

"Randi?"

"Yeah?"

"Do you think this whole place smells like wet, stinky socks?"

They both looked down at the stained mattress and cringed.

*   *   *

"So, why aren't we coolin' our heels in the 'big house' right now," Randi said in her best James Cagney voice. Scowling, she decided she sounded ridiculous, so she switched back to her normal voice. "Well, it turned out that jerk-off Bubba has a nasty little habit of accosting pretty women. A few hours after we were arrested, a prosecutor showed up and offered us a deal. He agreed to reduce both our charges to 'disturbing the peace,' if we agreed to 'hush up' about what Bubba did to Mac. Of course, we still had to pay a $1000 fine. Each." Randi shook her head in disbelief. "I nearly dropped dead on the spot when Mac refused to take the deal unless they gave her back her driver's license." Dark eyebrows rose. "Remember what I told you about people and their driver's licenses earlier?"

A grumpy look stole across the woman's face. "The fine pretty much cleaned out my bank account. I figured I had enough left for the trip down and meals. As far as the trip back…well, maybe I'd get lucky at the blackjack tables."

"We had already lost most of the day getting arrested and all, so we decided to get a motel room in Shitsville, USA." The squirrels looked skeptical. "Fine. Maybe that wasn't the name of the town, but it's my story, isn't it?"

*   *   *

"Maybe we should see if the jail will take us back," Mac commented, putting her suitcase on the nearest bed.

Randi grunted her agreement as she clicked on the bathroom light. Okay, she tried to click on the bathroom light, but it didn't work. "Cheap fuckers!" she mumbled.

"It's not like we can expect a lot for $29.99." Mac tested the dead-bolt and breathed a sigh of relief when the metal bar slid smoothly into place. She shivered a little as "Hotel California" played endlessly in her mind.

"I suppose you're right. I'm just going to shower and then go to sleep. I'm beat."

Mac nodded and decided to wait until morning to shower. She was nearly asleep when she heard a groan and another muffled curse from the bathroom. *No hot water, what a shock.* Still, at the end of the day they were free and alive (her expectations had been seriously lowered over the past several hours).

She was asleep when Randi finally emerged from the bathroom wrapped in a towel that nearly made halfway around her body. The driving instructor slipped into bed and tried not to think about whom or what had slept there the night before.

"Mac?"

Silence.

A little louder. "Mac?"

"Yeah," came the half-asleep response.

"You didn't forget the medal, did you?" Randi was dying to see it. Touch it. Caress it. Fondle…She began to consider the merits of another cold shower.

"Nope."

Yes! They were finally in the same room together! Randi licked her lips and eyed Mac's suitcase. "Can I see it?"

"Nope."

Randi nearly bolted from the bed. "Why the hell not?!"

Mac smiled wickedly. Randi didn't give her *nearly* enough credit. The nurse rolled over and stared at the pale blue eyes in the bed next to hers. "I mailed it to my parents' house. It'll be waiting for me when we get there."

Randi chuckled despite herself. "Oohhhh, you're a lot more clever than I gave you credit for…*Stalker.*"

"Randi?"

"What?"

"I *still* prefer, Mac."

PART II

CHAPTER *4*

"Our second day started out with me driving, and Mac being unusually quiet. True, we had fought the entire day before and ended up in jail, and now I was almost completely broke, but when we went to sleep in the Bates Motel things seemed friendly enough."

Randi rolled her eyes. "Now I know why men are always bitching. I never realized that women were so hard to figure out!"

The male squirrel grunted in agreement and received a vicious glare from his mate in response. He snuggled against his long-time partner and began tenderly grooming her in apology, all the while thinking that maybe this human wasn't as stupid as she first appeared. He wished he could explain to the woman that the way to a female's heart was to carefully remove all her fleas! People always missed the obvious.

"I think I'll call this part "Day Two: Thelma and Louise Got Off Easy". Randi looked expectantly at the squirrels who smiled...well, as much as squirrels can actually smile. The human *was* getting better at this title thing.

*   *   *

"What's wrong?"
"Nothing."

Randi frowned. "Fine…be that way then." If that's how her stalker wanted to play it, Randi could deal with it. What did she care if Mac was acting all broody and quiet? Let her stew. It would be nice to have a little peace and quiet on this trip.

Randi gripped the steering wheel tighter. "Are you *sure* nothing is the matter?"

"Yes." Mac was facing away from Randi, watching the autumn landscape fly by. She didn't need to bare her soul to Randi. The woman didn't even like her! Why should it matter that she *did* like Randi? Mac's brow creased. At least *most* of the time she liked her. But Mac knew she was just using Randi to get even with Sandra and her brother. *God, I'm a 'user' just like Sandra!* And wasn't Randi using *her* to get even with Sandra, and get that stupid medal?

They would each play their parts and then never see each other again. Mac didn't *need* Randi as a friend. But for some unknown reason she was starting to *want* her as one…badly. It was the kind of ache you feel when your heart irrationally wants something, but your head tells you that it's just not gonna happen. Like snow in July or Sandra mysteriously contracting the Ebola virus.

"Tell me about Sandra." Randi was getting desperate. This was the loudest silence she'd ever endured! After only one day together she needed to hear her stalker's voice, instead of the endless nothingness that filled the tiny Volkswagen. Randi mentally groaned. Did her health benefits include psychological therapy? How much was her medical deductible again?

"I don't want to talk about that two-timing, traitorous, lying, vindictive bitch!"

Wow! Mac really knew how to break a silence! "Same old Sandra," Randi sneered, relieved that Mac was saying *something*. "So what did she end up doing with her life?" Blue eyes danced with devilment. "Is she a gym teacher?"

Mac turned to face Randi, her own eyes flashing indignantly. "That is such a ridiculous cliché! Not *all* gay women are gym teachers! For Christ's sake, the woman has a degree in mathematics from one of the finest universities in the country. After college she went to work for some private company's think tank…umm…thinking, I guess."

"Making tons of money, no doubt." God, how Randi hated Sandra!

"No doubt." God, how Mac hated Sandra! "Anyway, she did that for a few years, until it no longer held her interest."

Randi didn't even want to ask. Sandra was probably working for some big computer or chemical company as an engineer. She probably had some fancy office with three secretaries at her beck and call. Bitch! But she had to know. "So what did she end up doing?"

A little smile edged its way onto Mac's lips. "She's a gym teacher."

*   *   *

"And then she laughed." Randi smiled just remembering. "I had seen her angry, and I'd seen her cry, but I had never *really* heard her laugh. It was a belly laugh that brought tears to her eyes and practically forced me to join in. Then it hit me. I liked her! I really…"

Oh no! Not the Sally Field imitation! The finest seeds on Earth weren't worth that! The squirrels breathed a huge sigh of relief when Randi bravely overcame the almost irresistible impulse.

"Oops. Sorry." The woman realized she had stopped tossing down seeds some time ago. With an apologetic smile, she threw out several seeds for each of her audience members.

The sky was beginning to darken, and the lights that lined the pathway in the park began to softly glow. Randi looked at Mac's apartment building, wondering which balcony was hers. Why didn't she just get up and walk over there? Randi fiddled with the bag of seeds. Later. Later was better. *Coward!! Chickenshit!!*

"Where was I?" Randi nodded. "Oh, right. After we laughed, the intensity level in the car seemed to drop a bit. Even though Mac was still being a little quiet, it was a more comfortable silence. The only problem was, it gave me time to think. When a person makes a monumentally bad decision, even if they aren't aware of how bad it is when they make it, the last thing they need is time to dwell on it. How was I going to pretend Mac was my girlfriend? Don't get me wrong. I was still willing to do **anything** it took to make Sandra suffer and earn that medal. But I was starting to get really nervous and, well, maybe just a *little* edgy." Randi held up her index finger and thumb, indicating an infinitesimal amount.

*   *   *

"How should I act?"

"Huh?" Mac put down her sack of corn nuts. "Act where?"

"While I'm at your parents house. Where else?!" Randi said exasperatedly. The tall woman stuffed her straw further into her soda and took another long sip.

"God, Randi, are you still freaked out about that?" Mac tossed another corn nut into her mouth and shrugged. "Just act like I'm your girlfriend. Don't think of me as a woman if it'll help."

Why was this so hard for Randi? It wasn't like she was going to ask her to screw her senseless right in front of Sandra. It was only a few harmless kisses for appearance's sake. She wasn't even going to use her tongue! Well, not unless she **had** to. And Mac certainly wasn't going to drag her hands across that firm stomach and up to those luscious, round, absolutely perfect…Mac's mouth and other, more southerly parts, began to water. She closed her eyes tightly. *STOP IT!*

"Hey? Are you still with me?"

"What? Oh…um…I was just thinking." A light blush crept its way across Mac's cheeks. The blonde shook her head and brought herself back to reality. "Look, Randi, you're used to going out with men. Just employ some acting skills. Think of this as a variation of 'faking it.'"

Randi's jaw dropped. "I have **never** faked it."

Mac slowly licked the salt off her fingers, all the while shooting Randi a sexy, knowing smile.

Randi felt her temper begin to rise. *Brat! How long has she been spying on me?! And why is she looking at me that way?* "Once," she blurted out in shame. "I only did it once!" Was there no end to her humiliation?! Randi knew she'd regret dating that cyclist. Everyone warned her about what that hard, pointy seat would do to his…

"Don't worry about it, Randi." Mac smiled sweetly. "You can just follow my lead."

"I'll bet," Randi snorted. Mac's face went from wanton and wily to 'the girl next door' in the blink of an eye, and the transformation sent Randi reeling.

"Randi, you don't trust me, do you?"

"Of course not!"

"I've never…"

"Don't get all high and mighty with me, 'Miss I Mailed the Medal to Las Vegas.'"

Mac winced. Sandra had said that Randi would do anything for the medal…that the woman was mentally unbalanced! Mac just didn't want to end up in a ditch somewhere between Buttscratch, Arkansas and Las Vegas. It was clearly nothing personal.

"Just remember our deal. No unnecessary contact."

The younger woman scowled. "I'll remember," she grumbled around a mouth full of nuts.

Randi watched with a mixture of fascination and embarrassment as Mac's tongue snaked out and tasted the salt on her fingertips. When Mac caught her staring, blue eyes quickly refocused on the road.

Pale brows lifted skyward. *Well…Well…Well…Maybe Randi wasn't made of wood after all.* "Do you want some, Randi?" she asked innocently. *The nurse loved subtext! Who didn't? It was fun and usually safe. Besides, she had only sworn off people named Bubba. C'mon, Randi. The ball's in your court.*

"You know, watching you eat those nuts is truly disgusting."

"And listening to you suck on that enormous Big Gulp for the last 100 miles hasn't been?" Mac shot back disappointed.

Randi swerved the car wildly, pulling into a gas station. "I need a bathroom break."

"What a shock."

"Shut up…*Stalker!*"

*   *   *

"She had finally pushed me too far. I was beyond furious. She was intentionally needling me with that 'faking it' comment. And then she started with the subtext. I hate subtext! It's a pathetic tease by people who can't make up their minds. Well, my mind was made up, dammit!"

Randi began to pace back and forth in front of the bench. The female squirrel shifted nervously. Was the human going to lose it? The dark woman was showing all the signs. She'd seen it happen before, when the stresses of their drone-like existence became too much to bear.

"She pushed, so I pushed back. Okay, maybe I pushed a *little* harder than she did." Randi was going to lift her fingers to indicate a small amount again, but she figured it wasn't worth it. Squirrels didn't even have fingers. What would the gesture mean to them?

*   *   *

Mac emerged from the 7-11 with a bottle of iced tea. She cringed when she thought about how many sit ups it would take to erase all the corn nuts she'd consumed. But she was powerless to resist their salty lure. They were road-trip food, and she was only human after all. Maybe she could get a jog in tonight after they stopped.

Sea-green eyes narrowed when Randi approached the car with a *Super* Big Gulp in hand, the side of the cup proudly proclaiming 64 ounces. The nurse schooled herself in patience. They would be in Las Vegas tomorrow and this would all be worth it. At least it had better be.

Randi offered to drive again and, not wanting her companion's car sickness to return, Mac agreed. The constant hum of the motor and the warm sun magnified by the car's windows soon had Mac dozing.

Eyes closed, the younger woman reached blindly into the back seat for her pillow. Then she smelled it. Burning rubber? Smoke? Maybe they had passed by a campsite or some homes with wood burning stoves. Then the smell got stronger and Mac reluctantly opened her eyes.

"What in the hell do you think you're doing?" Mac was shocked.

"What's it look like?"

"You don't smoke!" The younger woman searched her mind. No! She had stalk…er…trailed Randi enough times to know that she didn't smoke. The woman even insisted on eating in the 'No Smoking' sections of restaurants.

"I do now."

"It's a filthy habit!"

"I know."

"It will kill you!"

"But not today."

UGGGHHHH! "When did you start smoking?"

"About two minutes ago."

Mac tried to take a calming breath, but the tiny cab was completely filled with smoke, and she began to cough. Why hadn't Randi cracked a window? "Are you crazy?" she finally sputtered.

"I think the answer to that is obvious."

"That's it! You *don't* smoke, and you are certainly *not* smoking in *my* car. Stop now!"

Randi turned to face Mac. She took a painfully long drag on the cigarette and then slowly exhaled right in Mac's face. "No thanks," Randi coughed. "I'm starting…t…to warm up to th…this." In truth, Randi was near vomiting. But what the hell, it was for a good cause. This would teach Mac to tease her.

Mac waved her hand in front of her face, then made a wild grab for the cigarette. Randi jerked her head to the side causing Mac to miss her completely. "God dammit! Is this cigarette worth dying for?" Randi yelled, as she tried to keep the car on the road.

"You tell me," Mac screamed back, still trying to grab the burning butt. "Give it to me!"

"Never!" Randi roared.

In a lightning fast move, Mac was able to dislodge the cigarette sending it right into Randi's lap. Randi howled as it began to burn through her jeans.

"Get it off! Get it off!" the driving instructor screeched, as she tried in vain to keep the car out of the ditch.

"Hold still! Stop wiggling and drive!" Mac began digging between Randi's legs for the cigarette as she felt the car swerve out of control.

* * *

The male squirrel looked at his wife with frightened, black eyes, wondering if the humans made it. His heart began to pound. Cars were such vicious things! They were cruel, horrendous steel creatures whose only purpose was to mangle and...

Slap!

A tiny paw sent the male squirrel sprawling. "Snap out of it!" the larger female cried. When her mate's breathing returned to normal, she rolled her equally dark, beady eyes and let out a frustrated breath. Post-traumatic car syndrome was such a bitch! She lovingly wrapped her tail around her trembling mate.

"Do you guys need to get a room or something?" Randi asked, hoping she wasn't going to witness a private squirrel moment. "Should I keep going?" Hearing no objection she continued.

"The last thing I remembered was the car starting to roll, my Super Big Gulp putting out the cigarette, and Mac screaming something like 'but I didn't even get to kiss her yet!'"

* * *

Randi woke up to the feeling of gentle fingers running through her hair. Mac was pillowing her head in her lap, and she was lying in an empty cornfield about 25 feet from what was left of Mac's Volkswagen.

"Randi?"

"I think so," the older woman moaned.

"Thank God you're alright!" Mac hugged Randi fiercely. Tears were streaming down Mac's cheeks, and she had a nasty gash above her right eye.

Randi groaned as she tried to sit up. "Don't try to move, Randi. You've been unconscious for the past 15 minutes—let's just wait for an ambulance. I called 911 with my cell phone a few minutes ago."

The shorter woman's hands were shaking, and Randi grasped them with her own. "How...how did we get out of the car?"

"Don't you remember?"

Randi closed her eyes. She had a pounding headache. "The last thing I remember is being in the car." *And a cigarette that was about to start a forest fire in a place I'd rather not mention...* she added silently.

Mac nodded and removed one of her hands from Randi's so she could continue to stroke the head in her lap. The darker woman had an angry looking bump above her ear, and Mac was almost certain she had a concussion.

"You helped me get out of the car; I was pinned in. And you insisted on carrying me." Mac pointed to another cut just below her knee. "You were worried the car might explode. You collapsed a few feet from where we are now."

"Oh." Randi swallowed. "You make me sound like a hero or something," she said softly, a little embarrassed but glad both she and Mac *appeared* to be alive.

Randi wasn't about to take anything for granted. She could be dead and in hell at this very moment. And this could be nothing more than a satanic trick! Mac might whip out a big handful of corn nuts and start munching away at any second. Then Sandra would appear, and she and Mac would kiss, and then they would *both* begin eating corn nuts and smoking cigarettes.

OH GOD! Why didn't she go to church more when she had the chance? She didn't mean to have sex with that young priest in the confessional during the Christmas Eve service in 1993! If God didn't want her to have him, then why did He make the priest look exactly like Tom Selleck? He was practically gift-wrapped! Who could resist that? And the fact that they had *both* chosen not to wear underwear that day *had* to be a sign!

"Randi?" Mac prompted softly.

Confused eyes focused on Mac. "Hmm?"

"You faded out on me for a minute."

"I was just thinking." Randi stared at Mac for a long moment. "Do you have any more corn nuts with you?"

Mac shook her head. "No." The woman definitely had a concussion. "Are you hungry?"

"Nope. I was just checking."

Mac smiled. "Thank you for getting me out of the car. I'm a little claustrophobic, and I was already starting to freak out." Soft green eyes captured Randi's. "Just don't go getting too full of yourself, *hero*."

The brunette grinned. She'd never been a hero before. "Are you okay? That looks like a nasty cut." Randi reached up and gently traced the skin above Mac's eye.

"I'm okay. I don't think it's too bad. Head wounds just bleed a lot. But it'll probably need a few stitches."

Randi made a face. The thought of any medical procedure at all made her nauseous. She hoped that when the ambulance came they would knock her out with some good drugs. Or, at the very least, wait to stitch up Mac so that she wouldn't have to see it. The thought of the needle going in and out of her skin...Randi shivered.

Mac frowned a little. "I hope my forehead doesn't scar too badly."

"Does it matter?"

"Damn right it matters!"

"Why?"

"Well...well, it's obvious!"

"Not to me."

"But I'll look..."

"Just as pretty as you do now," Randi said, hoping Mac wouldn't consider the fact that *now* she had a gaping, bleeding head wound.

Hey! The driving instructor could be sweet when she wanted to be! Why does she keep a lid on the kinder, gentler side of her personality?

"Thanks, Randi," Mac said sincerely. "Are you sure it won't look too bad?" she asked skeptically.

"I'm sure," Randi assured quietly. Their eyes met and held for several long seconds before Randi grew too uncomfortable to hold the gaze and turned away.

Holy shit! The Volkswagen was nearly flat! They were lucky to be alive.

Mac followed Randi's eyes. *Damn. I hope I remembered to pay my car insurance last month.* "We're going to have to find another way to make it from here to Las Vegas."

Randi couldn't believe the younger woman still wanted to go through with their plan. She was obsessed and relentless! Nothing…not jail…not even a 'near death experience' could stop her! Sandra was clearly an idiot to give her up. Randi mentally added 'loser in love' to her enormous list of Sandra's unredeemable faults.

"We've still got to survive one more day together before we make it to Las Vegas, hero."

Mac's voice was teasing, but it somehow sounded different to Randi. The taller woman chuckled softly, enjoying the comforting motion of Mac's hand in her hair. "I think we're tempting fate, don't you?"

Mac shrugged and continued her tender stroking. "Unless this *is* our fate."

CHAPTER 5

"Are you ready to hear about Day Three?" Randi fished a piece of bubble gum out of her pocket and popped it into her mouth. Her throat was beginning to get a little sore, and the bitter wind had caused the tips of her ears to turn numb. She wished she had one of those disgusting cherry cough drops to sooth her throat…but gum would do.

The only people left in the park, other than the obligatory serial killer or two, were the diehard joggers. One or two of them would pass by occasionally, but Randi didn't even pause in her storytelling. She received several curious glances and outright stares. But she decided she didn't give a flying fuck if they *did* see her talking to the squirrels. She didn't care what anyone thought…well, with one exception.

"I've run out of peppy names, so I'll just call this "Day Three: Riding the Dog.""

The squirrels looked at each other. The human was right. That name really sucked.

*   *   *

Mac opened her eyes to find Randi asleep in a small hospital bed, bathed in morning sunlight. She had fallen asleep in the lounge chair in Randi's room, and every square inch of her body ached from the accident the day before.

For a few moments she silently watched the other woman's slumber, suddenly not at all anxious to figure out a way to travel the remaining 250 miles to Vegas. The fire in her belly—that's how she liked to describe her unquenchable need for revenge against Sandra…it had a more literary quality—had been steadily cooling since the day before. But Mac swore it was like an 80's perm: No matter *what* you did to it, it was still there! If it killed them both, and that was looking like a strong possibility, they would finish this trip together.

Randi had been diagnosed with a mild concussion, and the doctors had insisted she spend the night in the hospital for observation. The older woman had pitched a fit, but Mac was tired and irritable and simply not in the mood for a six-foot tall brat, who appeared to still be going through the 'terrible twos'. She put her foot down. They *were* staying.

Mac's forehead was now the unhappy home of seven stitches, but she had, thankfully, escaped a concussion. Randi had promised to keep her Frankenstein comments to a minimum. Mac, however, soon discovered that Randi's definition of 'minimum' differed dramatically from hers.

RING…RING…

Mac moved to answer the phone next to Randi's bed, hoping to allow her companion a little more time to sleep in, but an unsteady hand beat her to it.

"Hello." Randi held the phone slightly away from her ear and covered her eyes with her hand. After a few seconds she began quietly mouthing a colorful string of invective so inventive it completely astounded Mac. Even though the phrases were totally deplorable, Mac couldn't help but admire Randi's creativity. The younger woman finally believed what her mother told her as a child. Everyone had a special gift…you just had to find it. Granted, Randi's was a liiitle unusual…

"But I…Yes."

Mac swallowed nervously. Who could be calling Randi here? No one even knew where they were.

"My insurance was…"

"I know, but…FINE! You can just take your job and shove it right up your pruney, tight…" Randi suddenly stared at the phone in disbelief. "The jerk hung up on me! I can't believe it!"

"Who?"

"My former boss, the impotent little bastard."

Uh Oh. "Did you say 'former'?"

Randi nodded her head. She didn't know whether to be pissed or relieved. She hated that job anyway. Maybe this was just the jump-start her life needed? Maybe she could make lemonade from these lemons? Ha! What a crock of shit! She was jobless. And broke. And in the hospital with an insane, although at times surprisingly companionable, stalker. Now, if she would just start her period, her day would be perfect. Was it really only 8 a.m.?

"He fired you because you're in the hospital? He can't do that! How did he even know you were here?"

"My insurance card had expired. So that *good looking…*" Randi sneered the words, "…nurse you seemed to immediately bond with called my boss to get my policy numbers, and just happened to mention that I was on my way to Las Vegas, with a cute blonde, when I was in a car accident."

"She said I was cute? How sweet!"

Randi just glared.

Green eyes twinkled. "You aren't jealous, are you, *hero*?" *You are! Don't deny it.*

"You wish…*Stalker*," Randi snorted. *I am not in denial!*

Mac ground her teeth together. This 'stalker' business was getting sooo old. "Call me Mac."

As usual, Randi ignored her request. "I had to say I was sick to get this time off from work. I got fired for 'going on vacation' while I was supposed to be home, sucking down Pepto-Bismol."

Mac ran a nervous hand through her hair. "Oh God, I'm so sorry, Randi." She looked truly upset. "Maybe I can call your boss and explain? Maybe I can..."

A dark eyebrow rose. "And just what are you going to explain? Huh? I can hear it now...'Please don't fire Randi, Mr. Anson.'" Randi imitated Mac's grin and mannerism to a tee as the younger woman scowled. "'Randi couldn't come to work this week, because she was just too busy whoring herself out to me so that she could wear a 15-year-old, cheap-ass medal that never belonged to her anyway. Oh, and did I mention that her primary motivation for her absence is getting revenge on her high school nemesis, who betrayed their friendship for a scholarship, a pimply-faced, pubescent prick, and the chance to fuck on orange shag carpet?! Don't worry, I'll write her a note.'"

Mac winced. It sounded so pathetic coming from the *former* driving instructor. "I wouldn't exactly say 'whoring,'" the blonde mumbled sheepishly, her eyes trained on her feet. "I really am sorry." Watery orbs lifted to meet Randi's.

Jesus! She was going to cry again! "It's okay." Randi heard herself say. *NO!* she mentally whined. *That's not what I was going to say! I'm supposed to be mad at her for leading me down the primrose path to self-destruction.*

Then Randi's brain just seized up as she was struck right between the eyes with an epiphany. Why was she angry with the nurse again? It wasn't as if Mac forced her to go along with her plot. She went willingly...*very* willingly. It wasn't like she had the right to be jealous just because Mac made a friend overnight, literally. So why did it seem like every moment with Mac was a trial? The answer was staring her in the face like a zit on prom night. Because *she* made it that way! It was a blinding moment of self-realization that left Randi in a slack-jawed, wide-eyed state.

She liked Mac. She more than liked Mac, and from now on she was going to follow *that* feeling wherever it took her, instead of her petty mean streak that always got her into trouble anyway. It was time to focus on Sandra and work *with* Mac! She had been foolishly splitting her mental resources!

So Randi decided to do something she almost never did. She decided to give up. Give up fighting the urge to be near her stalker. Give up resisting the impulse to laugh and play with the younger woman. She refused to put a lid on the part of her that wanted to find Mac's quirks more endearing than annoying…Randi was going to have her cake and eat it too…or kill Mac trying. Let the shit hit the fan and the games begin!

Resolved, refocused eyes pinned Mac. "Don't worry about my job. I hated it anyway. You couldn't have known that nurse you spoke with would talk to my boss. Just let me get dressed so we can get out of here, okay?"

It was Mac's turn to stare. Wasn't Randi going to rant and blame her for getting fired? Why the hell not? After all, it *was* her plan and loose lips that were systematically destroying the older woman's life. "Who are you, and what have you done with Randi?"

Randi smiled. "Oh, it's me alright. I just decided to go with the flow. After all, we're partners in this, right?"

"You're just *now* figuring that out?"

BY ALL THAT IS HOLY!!! Couldn't Mac let Randi revel in her epiphany for even two damn minutes?! *I think I can. I think I can.* "Don't push it, *Stalker*," Randi snarled as she reached for her jeans. She stopped and stared at a unique looking hole. How *does* one cover a cigarette burn to the crotch?

Mac went to get Randi's nurse, feeling decidedly better. That nice, understanding Randi was really starting to give her the creeps.

*   *   *

"Ha! You didn't see that coming, did ya? You thought that I was going to be a hard-ass with Mac throughout this entire story, continually fighting against the friendship I was so obviously seeking. Ha! You didn't think I would even *try* to rise above our petty differences, did ya?"

Randi gloated as she blew an enormous bubble. A gust of wind suddenly blew the bubble back into her bangs. "Shit!" She began picking the gum out of her tangled locks.

The male squirrel looked disgusted. Why would the human be so foolish as to tamper with the teasing banter that was the cornerstone of the budding relationship? It added to the romantic tension and was just plain fun, and now it was gone! He didn't want to hear a story of self-discovery and acceptance. He wanted more flaming crotches, prison scenes and fights!

His mate blew out an annoyed breath. Males were such simpletons. If it weren't for the great sex she would…Well, never mind. Just because Randi accepted that she had feelings of friendship for Mac and decided to stop fighting them, didn't mean all the romantic tension had to disappear. It was clearly time for things to change and evolve! How could Randi ever grow emotionally if she wasn't brave enough to take that first step towards acceptance of a bone-deep bond? Actual success at civility didn't matter nearly as much as the sentiment behind the attempt!

Randi picked the last of her gum out of her hair and spat out the small bit that was left in her mouth. After slipping her gloves back on she turned up her collar against the cold evening air.

"We took a taxi from the hospital to the local Greyhound bus station and actually had a normal, pleasant conversation on the way there. I almost didn't know what to do with myself...."

* * *

Randi went directly to the cash machine in the bus station and cleaned out what was left of her checking account. Mac strolled over to meet her with their tickets in hand.

"Here you go." She passed Randi her ticket. The former driving instructor smiled her thanks and began counting out enough money to pay Mac. Pale brows knitted together. "Don't worry about it, Randi. The ticket is on me."

"I can't do that. I have enough money." The darker woman scowled a little and resumed her counting. She was no deadbeat. She could pay her own way.

"My dad sent me money for a plane ticket weeks ago," Mac lied, closing Randi's hand around the bills. "I'll still come out ahead in the end. Put your money away, okay?"

"But..."

"No buts." Mac glanced around the terminal for a distraction. "Look!" The blonde pointed at their bus. "We'd better go line up, or we won't get to sit together." Mac grabbed Randi's arm and began tugging her towards the line of people that were already forming by the bus door. She took a limping step to her bag and, with a grunt, settled the strap on her shoulder, only to have her hand covered by one of Randi's.

"I've got it." The older woman smiled and took the bag. "I'm sure your leg must still be hurting."

"Okay." Mac smiled back. "Thanks." This being friends thing was cool! Randi's smile was beautiful. The only problem was, now that

Randi wasn't acting like an ass all the time, Mac's attraction to the older woman was beginning to take on a life of its own.

Mac had been physically attracted to Randi since she first saw her in driving school. The nurse didn't know if she would survive being emotionally attracted to her as well. But what sweet torture! After a lifetime of being attracted to the *wrong* people, it felt wonderfully liberating to be attracted to someone that felt *right*.

It would be easy to fall in love with Randi. She could just tell. But the other woman didn't even know if she could *fake* being in love with her. It was all so frustrating! What could a man offer Randi that she couldn't? Okay, besides the ability to successfully pee off the side of a boat. And could that *really* be classified as a vital skill?

Mac had never seriously considered trying to seduce a straight woman before. What would be the point? But, oh, how she was tempted to try with Randi. She was rapidly coming to the conclusion that the pros outweighed the cons. Hell, Mac just wanted to be rapidly coming…And she wanted Randi there at the time. And naked. And covered with peanut butter…the creamy, not chunky. Mac laughed to herself, picturing the ultimate "Got Milk?" commercial.

"Thirsty?" Randi suddenly offered the nurse a sip of her pop.

Mac snapped out of her lust-induced trance and took the can from Randi's outstretched hand, carefully eyeing Randi's oblivious expression. Had Randi finally come to appreciate the delicate intricacies of subtext? Green eyes narrowed. Nah. Mac took a long swallow, then handed the can back to Randi. Shit! It was Dr. Pepper! The younger woman grimaced. Randi had horrible taste in wine *and* pop.

The two women settled into their seats, and Randi tried not to think about the hair that had touched the back of the seat before hers. Was it clean? Did they condition regularly? Did they have dandruff or worse…*Lice!* Was *it* the cause of that funky smell? No. Randi looked around as she not so discreetly sniffed. She was pretty sure the stench was coming from the seat in front of hers.

The tall woman shifted, trying to get more comfortable. When she tried to move her foot, she found it was stuck to the floor. *Eeewww! Please let it only be gum, please let it only be gum,* she mentally chanted.

Traveling by bus was just like she remembered it. Disgusting. Come to think of it...so far everyplace she'd been with Mac was smelly and gross. *I wonder why that is?*

The man in the seat in front of Mac and Randi suddenly turned around and stared at the women...and stared...and stared, all the while his mouth shaped in a big, dumb-ass grin.

"Nice tooth," Mac cheerily complimented.

Randi snorted her soda through her nose as she began choking.

The man's smile broadened before he turned his disturbing gaze on some other hapless passenger.

When the bus finally rumbled to life, two sets of tired eyes gazed out at the barren, arid terrain. It was much warmer here, and jackets and sweaters had given way to short-sleeved cotton shirts and t-shirts. Randi noticed a lonely cactus and briefly wondered what it would be like to be a desert snake. She'd ask Sandra tomorrow. Leaning against the window, she began to focus on Mac's homecoming.

"It's been forever since I've done this," Randi said, hoping to kill a little time with some easy conversation. She looked at her watch. It would be nearly bedtime before they reached Mac's parents' home. "My last bus trip was right after I finished high school. It was horrible. I never thought I'd be 'ridin' the dog' again."

And didn't that cyclist who picked you up from driving class count? Hmm? Ruff! For God's sake, he had one eyebrow! I rank lower than a unibrow? Mac closed her eyes and decided to sneak in a nap and try to think of ways to get Randi to go comparison shopping.

"Are you asleep?" Randi whispered after a few silent moments.

"Not yet," Mac answered, trying not to sound annoyed that Randi always seemed to want to talk when she wanted to sleep.

"What should I tell Sandra I do for a living?"

"Hmm?" Mac opened heavy eyelids and tried to focus on what Randi was saying. She hadn't thought about that. It would be better if Randi had some enviable job she could flaunt in front of the evil redhead. It would be better if Randi had *any* job. For a moment Mac considered just telling Randi to lie. But for some reason, something told her to tread lightly with this issue. "What do you want to tell her?"

Randi scratched her jaw. "Well, my current unemployment makes me even less desirable than I was as a driving instructor…"

"That's not true!"

"Are you saying I'm *more* desirable now that I'm *not* a driving instructor?" Randi's voice was increasing in volume.

"No!" Why was this conversation spiraling out of control? The afternoon had been going so well!

Randi suddenly looked a little embarrassed. "You're a nurse, and she's a teacher." Blue eyes rolled. "Okay, a *gym* teacher…but still…. I never even went to college." Mac was shocked to see pale, vulnerable eyes meeting hers. "Won't you be embarrassed to tell your folks that you're dating an unemployed…"

Mac held her palm up. "Just stop." She took Randi's hand, and this time the darker woman didn't even bat an eye. "I would *never* be embarrassed to take you home to my parents, no matter what you did…or *didn't* do for a living. I promise."

*   *   *

"I swear my heart actually skipped a beat." Randi swallowed. "Mac was offering me total acceptance, and she didn't even know me." Full lips curled into a lop-sided grin. "Then again, that probably had something to do with it. What she said should have made me feel great. But my emotions were so turned upside down, that I didn't know what I was feeling. The line between what was real and what wasn't was already beginning to blur, and we weren't even there yet. I did, however, decide one thing right there on that stinky Greyhound bus. It wasn't going to be nearly as hard to pretend to be in love with Mac as I had originally predicted."

CHAPTER 6

The bus broke down about 100 miles outside of Las Vegas, causing the women to arrive almost three hours late. Randi nearly cried when Mac decided it was too late to call her father for a ride from the bus terminal.

Of course, Randi hadn't spoken to her own dad in over 15 years, so she was hardly one to comment on Mac's relationship with her 'parental units'. She had, however, always considered men who were orphans highly desirable…less problems that way. She wondered how she would feel about her new 'girlfriend's' parents.

Another short bus and taxi ride later, and they were at Mac's parents' large lakefront home. The former driving instructor wasn't surprised to learn that Mac's parents didn't actually live in Vegas, but Boulder City, a sleepy little town on Lake Mead about an hour away from the big city. When it came to details, Mac had Randi on a need-to-know-basis. And, apparently, Randi didn't need to know shit.

* * *

"Ha, isn't that always the way with females?!" the male squirrel exclaimed. *Oops. Was that out loud?*

"Do you know what I was feeling as I approached the house?" Randi offered, slightly embarrassed. But hey, a storyteller has to go all the way if she wants her audience to really *know* what happened. "Other than nervous, I mean. I was actually excited." She looked at the squirrels expectantly, but they remained unmoved.

"I mean *excited*." Randi wiggled her eyebrows for emphasis as her voice took on a sensual edge.

If squirrels had eyebrows, two pairs would have shot straight up. "Ahh," they hummed in understanding. The male squirrel nodded his approval. The human didn't even have to use the "F" word to convey her thoughts. Her storytelling technique was improving. Now they understood. The human was one sick puppy. They had strongly suspected it before but…

"I know it sounds freaky. But I swear I was on fire! I was getting so close to something I had wanted for so long, that my body couldn't help but react. I could taste my revenge! And, no…it didn't taste anything like chicken."

*   *   *

The shorter woman directed them to a side door that seemed to lead to an addition to the house. Had Randi not been dead on her feet, she'd have wished they'd arrived in the daylight, so she could look around. Were Mac's brother and Sandra here? She'd ask Mac tomorrow, when her head stopped pounding. Concussions sucked.

The women made their way through the dark, silent house as quietly as possible. It was, after all, 2:30 in the morning.

"FUCK!! OUCH!!" Randi cursed in a muffled voice as she hopped around in a circle, clutching the toe she'd just stubbed on a small table.

"Shhh…" Mac lifted a finger to her mouth. "You're going to wake up the entire house," she whispered. The blonde couldn't help but smile. She felt like she was a teenager sneaking home after a late date. Not that she'd ever done that. But if she had…it would have been just like this.

The nurse pointed to the last room at the end of a very long, very dark hallway. "It's this way."

"This was your room?" Randi asked skeptically as she walked through the doorway. The room was small for what appeared, on the outside, to be such a big home. Randi looked around. It reminded her of a hotel.

There was a bed, lamp, and small dresser. That was it. Above the bed hung the obligatory landscape print whose colors matched the bedspread with an almost eerie precision. It was a nice room, the older woman decided…just not Mac. She pictured Mac as a knick-knack, stuffed animal, family portrait, borderline 'Precious Moments' kind of person. Randi made a face, sincerely hoping she was wrong about that last part.

Mac flopped back on the bed exhausted. "No," she laughed. "Does this look like a room I would live in? It's just a spare guestroom. There's actually a much nicer one, but my guess is my asshole brother and his hussy got dibs on it."

Randi shook her head, secretly pleased that she was beginning to know her stalker's tastes…and they didn't run along the lines of clean but sterile. The brunette tilted her head toward the hall, not wanting to open the door to a conversation about Sandra. At the moment, she was simply too tired to put forth as much effort as a really good, soul-consuming hatred required. "Which one was yours then?"

"None of them. I've never lived in this house. My folks sold their business and moved down here about six years ago. I grew up back home."

That made sense. Randi wondered why Mac and her brother had both ended up in the same city, so far from Nevada.

The smaller woman curled up into the fetal position and grimaced, her face contorted in distress. Randi sat down next to her on the bed and cupped her chin, turning Mac's face towards hers. "I hurt inside! Don't you?" Mac suddenly blurted out.

A dark eyebrow shot upward. "It was that hot dog, wasn't it? Like I really would have eaten one of those," she snorted.

The blonde could only nod. Randi had warned her. But she couldn't resist!

"What kind of idiot buys a hot dog from one of those spinny thingies at a gas station? Ick! It had probably been rolling around in its own grease for weeks before you bought it. My guess is that you'll die."

"But I was starving!"

Randi simply shrugged. "So you'll be a full corpse."

Uh Oh... That reminds me. "Thanks so much for the words of comfort." Mac moaned a little and turned pitiful eyes towards Randi's suitcase, knowing the older woman had some Tums hidden away in her bag.

"Fine, you big baby. I think I have something in my suitcase that will settle your stomach."

"Thanks, *lover*," Mac purred.

"Ha ha." Randi passed over two different colored tablets. "Chew."

Mac frowned and almost asked for matching flavors but was stopped by a 'don't push it' look. "Okay...Okay," she grumbled around the horribly chalky tablets.

Randi rolled her eyes. "Do you want me to get you some water to wash them down?"

"Nah...I'll be fine," Mac said as Randi flopped down onto the bed next to her with a groan.

Oh God! It was so comfortable. The brunette resolved to never leave this spot.

Mac rolled over to face Randi and propped herself up on one elbow. "Thanks for the medicine."

"Sure."

Here goes. "Randi?"

"Hmm?"

"We didn't ever discuss what my parents do for a living, did we?"

"Not that I remember. I figured they were probably in the medical field, like you and your brother. Let me guess. Your father is Dr. Kevorkian, and your mother is discovering a cure for Jock itch as we speak, right?"

"Umm...Not exactly." Mac hesitated long enough for Randi to turn her head and face her. Mac swallowed. "Well, you see…"

Randi noticed a flash of uncertainty in Mac's eyes. "They must do something pretty important. This house is really big." It had taken the women five minutes just to walk up the driveway. Mac looked down at the bedspread and began to pick at the floral pattern beneath her fingertips. Randi's curiosity was piqued. Were they criminals or lucky gamblers? Was the witness protection program this well-funded?

"Mom is a minister."

Randi looked confused, so Mac repeated herself. "You know, a preacher…religion…that sort of thing."

"Oh." Randi scowled. She had no use for organized religion and considered its leaders little more than charlatans. But Mac didn't seem the repressed ultra-religious type or the classic, whorish preacher's daughter. But then again, she was a stalker. Randi smiled, more than happy to blame that little character flaw on a religious upbringing.

"Does that bother you?" Mac said a little defensively. The nerve! It's not like she'd told Randi her mother was a lawyer!

"She doesn't lead one of those cults where all the members have shaved heads and look like Mr. Clean, does she? Heh. Oh no! Please tell me she's not a televangelist. Those vultures should be shot."

"You are truly obnoxious." But Mac found herself fighting back a smile. "Do you ever actually listen to yourself?"

"I wasn't talking to *myself*." Randi's lips curved into a devilish grin. "I was talking to *you*."

"No, she's not a televangelist. And she has nothing to do with my dad's lack of hair." Mac paused. *At least I don't think so.* "She ministers to a small congregation here in Boulder City."

Randy yawned. "That's not *so* bad. You had me thinkin' there was something to really worry about for a minute. Is your dad a preacher too? Or does he just hand out those little brochures proclaiming the end of the world?"

"No." Mac began to fidget and Randi narrowed her eyes.

"It can't be that bad." Oh, yes it could. And the darker woman knew it too. But, hell, she was *trying* to be sensitive. Randi had always found that sensitivity required an inordinate amount of lying.

"He's a mortician, and the front of the house is a funeral parlor," Mac said in a rush as she sat back and waited for the impending explosion.

She wasn't disappointed.

*   *   *

The male and female squirrel looked at each other with horror in their eyes and simultaneously exclaimed, "Ewwww!"

Randy snorted, correctly interpreting the gesture. "Tell me about it." The woman tossed out a few more seeds.

"Even a lawyer would have been better than this! Well…except for Johnny Cochran." Randi shivered at the thought. "And she didn't have to call me a big scaredy cat."

The male squirrel's eyes went glassy, and he began to tremble.

"Not again," the female muttered as she clutched her shaking mate. First cars, now cats. Was the human trying to send her mate over the edge? Didn't she realize how fragile the male mind was? Did she know how many acorns it took to get a good therapist?!

*   *   *

Randi flew off the bed like her butt was on fire. "Holy shit! Are you telling me there are dead people in the house with us?!" Blue eyes darted around wildly. *Escape, escape!* her mind screamed.

Mac felt a sinking sensation in the pit of her stomach. "Well, there might not be," she offered hopefully. "It all depends on…" She stopped when she could see that Randi wasn't really listening. She sighed. No one ever took the news well. She had always grown up living alongside or even above a mortuary—and always suffered because of it. Her slumber parties were *not* the parties of choice.

"Why didn't you tell me about this before?" Randi demanded. God, Mac was going to be the death of her yet!

"Would you have agreed to stay here?"

"No! And I'm not staying here now!"

"Oh, yes you are, you big scaredy cat!" Mac jumped to her feet and punctuated each word with a sharp poke in the chest.

"Owww!" Randi clutched her breast with a shocked look on her face. Who knew her stalker was so physical?

"Oops, sorry." Mac smiled sheepishly. "I could rub it for you and make it feel all better?" A sweet, hopeful lilt colored her voice.

Randi opened her mouth and then shut it as Mac began blushing furiously. *She's pretty when she does that.* Then Randi's own thought had her blushing as well. *Oh Christ!* "Is that the treatment you offer *all* your patients, nurse?" No, Mac was definitely not repressed.

"Only the ones with fabulous…" A firm hand over the blonde's mouth muffled her words.

An elegant eyebrow arched in a way that Mac was starting to consider more sexy than menacing. "Thanks." The eyebrow dropped. "But don't think I've forgotten about this place being a funeral parlor." Randi was trying to maintain her 'angry face'. But by Mac's suddenly contented look, she knew she was blowing it big time. Or maybe the Tums were finally kicking in. Randi couldn't be sure.

Mac scrunched up her face and sat back on the bed. "I know. I know. It's kind of creepy, huh?" But it really wasn't creepy at all to Mac. She had lived this way for the first 18 years of her life, then happily escaped to college. Now, over 10 years later, she worked in a place where death was a common occurrence. Death was just a natural part of life…granted, the *very last* part…

Randi nodded. She didn't want to look like a wuss. But damn, these weren't spiders they were talking about. They were corpses! Oh God! Wasn't a mortuary where they drained people's blood? Randi's face turned ghostly white.

"Here, sit down before you pass out." Mac guided Randi back onto the bed, and the older woman closed her eyes.

The former driving instructor's headache was making her feel sick, and she was so tired, and she was in bed with a woman who wanted to rub her boobs, and there were dead bodies, probably in the next room and…

"Stop thinking so much, Randi," the blonde ordered softly. "Just relax." Why did Randi have to work herself into a tizzy? It's not like they would actually see any corpses…at least until tomorrow. Mac made a mental note to remind her dad that not everyone appreciated his 'shop talk', and that Randi wouldn't want a tour of the embalming room or crematorium.

"I'm tired," Randi slurred, soaking in the soft feeling of the bed, already nearly asleep.

"I know. Just rest, hero. Your head will feel better in the morning. I'm going to get some blankets and bed down on the floor." Mac turned toward the dresser.

"No."

Mac turned back. "What?"

"I mean…You don't have to…Umm…You can stay up here." Randi opened one eye and rolled it towards Mac. "Just no funny stuff, okay?"

she got out before her eye closed again, and she burrowed a little deeper into the soft, comfortable bed.

Mac smiled warmly. And it wasn't just from the Tums. "Okay. Thanks, Randi. In the morning we can talk about…" The nurse stopped when she was interrupted by her companion's light snores. "Never mind."

Mac thought about waking Randi and getting her to put on some pajamas, but the older woman looked so comfortable, she didn't have the heart to disturb her. She changed into shorts and a thin T-shirt before covering Randi with a spare blanket.

With a quiet click the room went black, and Mac slipped into bed alongside Randi, inordinately pleased that her mother hadn't exchanged the full-sized beds for King-sized, as she'd been threatening to do for years.

Randi turned in her sleep, causing her arm to flop across Mac's mid-section. "Uuff! Thanks a lot, Randi," the younger woman muttered. She didn't want Randi to wake up and freak out because they were touching, so Mac carefully moved the limp arm until it was nestled between them. Regretfully, she began to let go when a hand grabbed hers and held it firmly. Mac's broad smile went unseen in the darkness as she closed her eyes.

*　　*　　*

"Yeah. I know. I'm busted. I woke up when she put the blanket on me. But she was so sweet the way she tucked me in. My own parents never did that. Not even once!"

Randi suddenly felt self-conscious over what she believed was an admission that was irrelevant to her story. She jumped to her feet and began stomping in the muddy puddles around the bench, sending muddy, icy water splattering in all directions.

"Why is she doing that? I've seen miniature humans do the same thing," the male squirrel hissed to his mate.

"She's an idiot?"

"Uh huh."

Randi walked around behind the bench and rested her elbows on its back, staring intently at her audience, who appeared to be snuggled up together and willing to stay with her for the duration of her tale. No matter *how* she decided to burn off a little tension. She wondered briefly if they were a 'couple'. They looked so content, just sitting there…together…waiting for her to continue.

Jesus! Now she was envying rodents and their interpersonal relationships? *I am one sick puppy!* But the simple thought of what *they* might have that *she* didn't made Randi's heart hurt. Suddenly, she hurt for all the things she wanted, whether she understood why she wanted them or not.

"I *am* a wuss and a scaredy cat!" she exclaimed loudly, sending a puff of fog billowing upward.

The squirrels shrugged. "True."

"When I finish here, I'm going to march right into that apartment complex and pound on every door until I find Mac!" Randi asserted boldly.

The male squirrel whispered to his mate, "Think she'll realize she could just look on the mailboxes and find out which apartment is Mac's?"

His mate chuckled. "I'd have to say 'no' at this point. She is *only* human after all. Deductive reasoning is usually beyond their grasp."

A layer of thin ice had started to form on the puddles that Randi had neglected to stomp through. Even the joggers had all gone inside for the evening. Randi looked around. The park seemed to be hers alone.

An icy rain began falling again as the temperature hovered around freezing. Randi sat back down on the bench. "I'd better get right to the part where I first saw Sandra, so I don't freeze to death. It's *really* starting to get cold." Randi pulled a tissue from her coat pocket and wiped her slightly runny, frozen nose.

"Finally!" the male squirrel stated. "I was really beginning to wonder how much longer she was going to try and drag this out."

PART III

CHAPTER 7

Mac and Randi didn't emerge from the bedroom until nearly 10 a.m. Both women felt worlds better after a good night's sleep, but Mac still had to assure Randi that she wouldn't see any dead people on the way to the kitchen, before the older woman would agree to leave the bedroom. She also spent several tense moments trying to convince the brunette that the house did *not* look exactly like the one in "Nightmare on Elm Street." Which was bullshit…because it did. Mac shivered. *Damn that freaky Freddy Krueger!*

Randi followed Mac down the long hallway. Blue eyes took in the lovely home with a mixture of nervousness and dread, as Randi's stomach did flip-flops. This was it. Any minute now she'd see that skinny bitch, Sandra. Convincing Mac's family that she and her stalker were a 'couple' was one thing…but Sandra *knew* her. *Shut up, dumbshit,* she told herself. *You knew her, too.* Things change…sometimes *big* things…sometimes *really big* things.

Mac reached behind her, finding Randi's hand; she lightly squeezed it as she led the taller woman down a small set of stairs.

Randi swallowed nervously but returned Mac's gentle, comforting pressure. "Where is everyone?"

"I don't know. Maybe Mom had to go to the church this morning. But I smell coffee."

The women followed their noses to the kitchen to find a short, blonde man sitting alone at the table. The man looked up at Mac and smiled smugly. Randi knew instantly that this little shit had to be Mac's brother. How could he bring Sandra, the slut, here to flaunt in Mac's face?

Randi shook her head. Her dad may have locked her out of the house when she was still a teenager, and, sure, her mom occasionally forgot to make sure her skirt wasn't tucked into her nylons before exiting a public restroom, but, dammit, even *they* looked liked winners compared to Mac's piss poor excuse for a brother.

Mac stopped dead in her tracks, her eyes locked onto ones barely a shade lighter than her own.

"Hello, *Morag*," the man sneered.

Randi looked at Mac. Her name wasn't Mackenzie?

Mac's body went rigid, and her hands shaped into fists. "Hello, *Angus*," she sneered back.

Randi made a disgusted face. Just how twisted were Mac's parents?

"Call me Mac!" the siblings shouted in unison.

Randi stepped in between the brother and sister, wondering if they'd come to blows. Mac's face was scarlet and Angus' forehead had sprouted an angry, pulsing vein. "Calm down, Mor…" Mac flashed Randi a look that would melt steel. "…err…sweetheart," she finished lamely.

Mac's anger instantly drained away at Randi's words, even if they were just for show. "Okay, *honey*," she said in a voice so sweet and sincere that Randi's heart lurched even as her head spun.

"Ahemmm!" Angus cleared his throat loudly. "Aren't you going to introduce me to your amazon friend?" The man stood up to his full 5'6" height, raking his eyes over Randi as if she were on the auction block. "I'm *Doctor* Mackenzie, but you can call me Mac," he said to Randi, not waiting for his sister's answer.

Mac rolled her eyes. "You can call him shithead, like I do. Or *Doctor* Shithead…" green eyes twinkled "…like his staff at the hospital does."

Randi barely swallowed a laugh. Meeeeeoooooow! Mac was vicious! The former driving instructor gave Angus a thorough once over before turning to her partner, a slender, dark eyebrow at its zenith. "Proctologist?"

Mac just smiled adoringly.

Angus glared at his sister, unable to get any closer to her because of the tall, athletic body blocking his path. Had Morag been hanging out in those biker bars again? He could definitely picture this bitch in leather. Oh yeah. Lots of tight, black leather.

Angus tore his eyes off Randi, more than a little envious of his younger sister. What could Morag offer this drop-dead gorgeous woman that he, a virile, manly *doctor*, couldn't? He sighed. Tits. It had to be the tits!

"Gee, Sis…you're not still bitter about Sandra, are you?" Angus gibed, knowing damn well that she was. "I really thought you'd be over that by now."

"Who?" Randi inquired innocently.

"Nobody important, honey." The blonde took a step forward and wrapped her arm around Randi's waist. The taller woman reciprocated the gesture, and Mac didn't try to stifle her contented sigh at the affectionate touch.

"So, *shithead*…" Mac said, enjoying the angry look on her brother's face, "…where are mom and dad?"

"Outside," he snorted, not offering any other information.

Randi gave Mac a quick squeeze, causing her to exhale explosively. "Okay…Jeeze," Mac hissed under her breath. "Angus?"

"Huh?" Grumpy blue eyes looked up from a medical journal they were pretending to read.

"Where are you hiding my *sloppy seconds*? I haven't seen her yet this morning?"

A huge grin split Randi's face. OH BABY! If she were into chicks, Mac would be the 'one'!

"You wouldn't be talking about me, now would you, Morag?"

*   *   *

The squirrels' eyes widened with anticipation, the steady sprinkle of icy, cold rain doing nothing to dampen their enthusiasm. They were enthralled. The story's villain had finally arrived.

"Bitch-slap her!" the male squirrel cried, no longer able to contain his excitement.

"Shut up, fool!" his mate hissed, smacking him in the back of the head and sending him sprawling onto his rounded stomach. "You know I'm opposed to violence!"

The female squirrel flicked her paws in the universal "continue" motion. "Go on, go on," she urged the human.

Randi sneezed and reached into her pocket for more tissue. Empty. "Crap," she muttered.

The dark-haired woman sighed as she watched another apartment go black. Were people going to bed already? She didn't look at her watch. It didn't really matter what time it was.

"And there she was, just like I remembered...."

*   *   *

Mac and Randi turned as one to face the freckled, painfully-thin red-head. "As a matter of fact, I was referring to you. Hello, Sandra," Mac said, trying to keep her voice even.

The nurse watched with supreme satisfaction as the color drained from Sandra's face. *That's right, bitch. It's Randi! Shit a solid-gold brick!*

Mac felt a wave of tension roll through Randi's body. She gingerly moved the hand that was wound tightly around her partner's waist and began softly stroking the taller woman's rigid back. *C'mon. Don't lose it now, Randi.*

"Hello, Sandra. Long time no see," Randi drawled, as she desperately tried to silence the eerily robotic chant that was running through her mind. *She...must...die...She...must...die...*

"Ra...Ra...Randi?" the redhead stuttered in a stunned voice. Oh God! This couldn't be happening, could it? Like a bad penny, or an unusually spooky 'third cousin' who shows up at all the family reunions and eats and eats and eats, but no one actually knows who he is, Randi was back.

The lanky woman took a small step forward towards Sandra. Still in shock, the gym teacher stumbled backwards so quickly that she ran into the kitchen counter. The cabinet stopped her lower body, but her momentum kept her upper body in motion, causing her head to slam against the cabinet door with startling force. Brown eyes rolled back in their sockets as the skinny woman crumpled into a heap on the floor.

"Stand back! I'm a *doctor*!" Angus proclaimed as he rushed over to his fallen girlfriend.

Mac and Randi just rolled their eyes.

"Any chance that she's dead?" Randi whispered, watching with amusement as Angus tried to examine Sandra.

"Like we're *that* lucky," Mac snorted.

"True."

Randi fought back a myriad of emotions as she studied her sworn enemy...the woman who changed her life forever...the woman she despised above all others...the woman who betrayed Mac. *What the hell?* Randi was shocked to find her anger at Sandra for hurting Mac equal to, if not greater than, her anger over the sabotage of her own future.

Sandra groaned and slapped away Angus' inquiring hands.

"Angus, do you need me to get you some KY jelly and a rubber glove?" Mac offered helpfully.

"What are you doing here?" Sandra asked Randi as she grasped Angus' arm and pulled herself to her feet. The redhead regained her composure with lightning speed and went on the offensive. "The last time I saw you, you were being sentenced to seven days in jail and 300 hours of community service," she snarled.

Mac tried not to look surprised. Jail? Randi was a criminal? *Not that I can really be critical,* she mused wryly. The thought of Randi and a pair of handcuffs temporarily derailed Mac's mind. *If she asked me to bend over and pick up her bar of soap, I'd sure as hell be happy to do it!*

Randi looked as though she might reach out and strangle Sandra on the spot, so Mac answered for her. "She's with me."

Sandra curled her fingers into quotation marks (the most annoying gesture in the history of mankind). "*With* you. Honey, you're going to have to try a lot harder to get me to believe that! I know her and she's *not* gay!"

"I would have said the same thing about you," Randi interjected. "And maybe it *wasn't* me that broke into your car!"

Sandra narrowed her deep, brown eyes. "Do you expect me to believe a common thief would steal it, glue orange shag carpet to every possible surface, and then return it?!"

Randi wisely decided to drop the subject of her 'innocence'. "Just remember, Sandra, that restraining order you got against me ran out years ago," Randi reminded her with a menacing look; a look that was designed to wreak havoc on Sandra's bladder control.

Despite her best efforts not to, Sandra twisted a little.

That's right. Be afraid. Be verrrry afraid.

Angus scowled, unable to follow the thread of the conversation. He had given up trying to figure out exactly who this 'Randi' person was. Someone would tell him...eventually.

"She *does* like men!" he finally exclaimed petulantly, several seconds too late for it to really make sense in the conversation.

Mac stood nose-to-nose with her brother. "That *still* doesn't explain why she's with you."

Sandra stole a glance at Randi. Could she and Mac actually be 'together'? This had to be a trick. But what if it wasn't? Sandra watched as Randi gazed at Mac with warm, puppy-dog eyes. It was true! Randi was gay! How could she not have noticed?

Sandra kicked herself repeatedly. For a night with the raven-haired beauty, whom she hated more than Kathy Lee Gifford and Martha Stewart combined, she'd even risk being thrown off the *Doctor* Dumbass gravy train.

"Your brother is right, Morag." Sandra turned to Mac and curled her fingers into quotation marks (*still* the most annoying gesture of all time). "I don't like women in 'that' way."

Mac raised an eyebrow as she cocked her head to the side. "Oh really?" Her hands went to her hips. "You could have fooled me. Especially when you had your face parked between my…"

"Morag, dear, you finally made it!"

A petite woman in her late fifties came barreling into the kitchen. "How's your head?" Motherly hands inspected Mac's forehead and placed a gentle kiss on the bandage. Then she looked around the room at all the angry, sour faces. "Did Angus fart again?"

Randi could only stare at the woman. This was Mac's mother? The *minister*? Ever since Gopher from the 'Love Boat' had been elected to congress, Randi suspected God had a wicked sense of humor. Now she had proof.

"Oh, I've missed you!" Mac pulled the tiny woman into a fierce hug, temporarily forgetting about Angus and Sandra.

"Same here, daughter," Mac's mother added, kissing her again.

Randi stood by awkwardly as the mother and daughter embraced. The former driving instructor immediately liked Mac's mom, who exuded warmth and a refreshing honesty. But most of all she liked the way she greeted Mac. Randi firmly believed her mom could be like that too. But only if she *really* increased her meds.

Mrs. Mackenzie finally untangled herself from her daughter and approached Randi. Smiling, she held out her hand. "I'm Belle. You must be Randi. I've heard so many wonderful things about you."

Randi nodded as her face colored. She glanced at Mac, who had her eyes firmly trained on her shoes and a slight grin tugging at her lips. "It's nice to meet you, ma'am."

Sandra groaned a little, trying to draw everyone's attention away from Randi and garner a little sympathy for her bruised head. Even Angus' eyes were riveted on the striking woman.

Belle completely ignored the gym teacher. That scarlet-haired tramp wasn't nearly good enough for her lovely daughter, Morag. Belle looked over at Angus and rolled her eyes. He, on the other hand, was lucky to have a companion that didn't require an air pump or batteries.

In the darkest corner of her heart, Belle clung to the flickering hope that indeed there *had* been a mix-up at the hospital, and Angus was not a blood relative. The Lord truly did work in mysterious ways. Love and $175,000 had allowed Angus to become a doctor. Who knew that Tijuana had a medical school? Of course, that meant her true son, no doubt cruelly named Cletus, was probably the moderately successful assistant manager of a dirty bookstore, or the perpetual "guinea pig" for one of those politically correct shampoo companies that doesn't test its product on animals. Belle said a prayer.

The kitchen suddenly became even more crowded, when a handsome, bald man in his middle sixties joined the fray.

"Daddy!" Mac flung herself into her father's outstretched arms.

"Hi, Sweetheart," he greeted his daughter in a booming voice. Randi immediately detected a slight accent that she associated with that fruity midget from the 'Lucky Charms' commercials.

Mac proudly introduced Randi, who stood silently as Mr. Mackenzie seemed to evaluate her...*judge* her. The tall woman squared her shoulders and lifted her jaw. Was she, an unemployed, broke, former driving instructor, worthy of his little girl? A light sweat broke out across her brow. Could he be fooled? *Oh, the pressure!!!!*

"I love Melissa Etheridge! I swear it!" Randi finally blurted out, buckling under his withering gaze.

Mac closed her eyes. Randi had been doing so well.

Mr. Mackenzie raised bushy, gray eyebrows. Huh? Oh well, if his baby loved this woman, that was good enough for him. Anyone was better than that skinny, opportunistic slut, Sandra. He finally extended his hand. "My name is Sean. But you can call me..."

"Mac," Randi immediately supplied as she grasped the stout man's hand in a firm handshake.

Sandra's face contorted in rage. That ghoul had never said *she* could call him Mac. *And I toured that horrific embalming room!* she seethed.

"C'mon, Randi. Let me show you my boat, before I get too busy this afternoon." Belle grabbed Randi and began dragging her out of the kitchen. Randi looked helplessly back at Mac, who was being herded out the other door by her father.

How was she supposed to make Sandra suffer, if they weren't even in the same room? She didn't drive 1500 miles to see some damn boat! "Um...Belle, shouldn't we invite Sandra to come along too?" Randi asked as Belle practically pulled her out of the kitchen.

"Hell, no! Why would I want to spend any time with that horrible, scrawny woman?"

"Umm…. Umm…" *Oh no! I can't think of a single reason! I need time to think!* Deep in her soul, Randi knew that her decision against becoming an air-traffic controller had been the right one.

With hate filled eyes, Sandra watched Randi leave the kitchen. Oh, how she had underestimated Mac (she only called her Morag to her face to annoy her). She should have realized the blonde had hard feelings about their break up, when she stepped on her super deluxe health meter—okay…scale—and noticed that taped over the high-resolution digital screen was a piece of paper that read, "YOU ARE ONE *FAT BITCH!* DIE! DIE! DIE! DIE! DIE!"

*   *   *

"I spent the next three hours 'looking' at Belle's boat, 'The Deliverer', drinking homemade strawberry wine, and talking about Mac. Belle explained that Mac's dad wanted to help her pick out a new car, so they probably wouldn't be home until late afternoon, when the rest of the family and friends would arrive for the gathering."

"No one actually called it a 'party'." Randi lifted an eyebrow at her audience. "But it was one. I asked Mac about it later, and she explained that if there were no balloons, it couldn't be a party." Randi shrugged. "I had to take her word on that since I didn't have a freakin' clue what she was talking about."

"I should have been angry that we were almost immediately separated. I mean, we were on a schedule here. But how could I begrudge her dad for wanting to help and spend time with her? I felt exactly the same way." Randi had hoped the bald mortician would talk Mac out of getting a Volkswagen. How many Fahrvergnügen jokes could one woman be expected to know?

Randi coughed, uncomfortably aware that her sore throat was getting worse. The cold wind was making her eyes feel dry and itchy, so she closed them for several long moments. She burrowed her face into her coat, and her audience noticed that her breathing seemed to slow. Except for the occasional gust of wind, the park was now silent.

"Is she asleep?" the male squirrel asked.

"Why don't you jump up on the bench and get a closer look," his mate suggested, knowing she wouldn't do it herself.

"Ha! Are you crazy? Isn't it obvious that she's demented? She's a convict, for God's sake!" The male squirrel folded his furry arms across his chest and scowled. "Besides, I don't appreciate the way she is portraying the males in this story. We are *not* all arrogant, farting simpletons!"

His mate was impressed by his uncharacteristically impassioned speech.

The male squirrel danced eagerly. "I just wish she'd hurry up and continue. I can't wait until she tells us who this Morag person is!"

The female squirrel hung her head and sighed. *Why did Mother always have to be right?!*

Randi suddenly lifted her head. With an irritated hand, she rubbed her eyes, which were now conspicuously wet.

The squirrels looked at each other. Was she crying? They couldn't tell.

The woman cleared her voice a little before she continued. "I got a ton of great 'blackmail' material about my stalker. But best of all, I found out that both Belle and Mac's dad *hate* Sandra."

"Belle believes that Sandra made a pact with Satan, where she gets to live forever in return for bringing misery to the Mackenzie family." Randi's watery eyes glistened in the hazy lamplight. She smiled weakly. "Belle is a very interesting person."

The brunette turned sideways on the bench and stretched her long legs out in front of her, soaking the back of her already damp jeans. "Belle was right. I didn't see Mac again until the back yard was full of people, and a small band began the torturous process of tuning their instruments…or playing…I wasn't quite sure which. Doesn't that sound like a damn party to you?!" Randi snorted.

The squirrels nodded. It was party time.

CHAPTER *8*

It had been a glorious day of torturing Sandra. After Randi was finally able to convince Belle that she'd adequately 'appreciated' her boat, she became Sandra's annoying shadow. The brunette followed Sandra around the house from room to room without ever actually confronting her. By early evening the redhead was fit to be tied, and Randi was in heaven! Mac's plan was working better than she'd even hoped!

Sure, Sandra was skeptical that she and Mac were a real couple…but with each passing moment Sandra was starting to doubt herself more and more. And Randi gleefully exploited these doubts. Should the former driving instructor be enjoying this so much? Of course! Some days were simply a bitch…and Randi had waited, not so patiently, for 15 long years to be that bitch.

During the few times the women did engage in brief conversation, Sandra mostly threatened to hire someone to kill Randi, and the taller woman helpfully pointed out that gym teachers didn't make enough money to hire hit men. But hey, at least they didn't have to work summers!

Other than that, Randi almost exclusively talked about Mac. She even thanked Sandra for foolishly moving along to Angus and clearing the path for her. Blue eyes twinkled when she saw how that dig especially was right on target. *Enjoy the money, stupid bitch, 'cause otherwise you got screwed, and you know it! There are no second chances with Mac for you!*

Randi's thoughts turned dark. Mac wouldn't go temporarily insane and decide she wanted Sandra back, would she? No. That wouldn't happen. Randi wouldn't let it.

* * *

"Oohh, hatred mixed with jealousy! This story is taking a turn for the better. I just know there's going to be a lover's triangle and then a gory, bloody murder!" the male squirrel shouted gleefully. If he wasn't going to get any more flaming crotches, murder was certainly the next best thing. A prison scene would surely follow!

"Mmmm.... No," his mate stated flatly. "Haven't you been listening? Randi is jealous because she is developing *real* feelings for Mac."

The male scrunched up his face. "Huh?" Did that mean no murder?

The female squirrel let out a disgusted breath. "Just listen..."

* * *

Sandra tried to escape Randi by fleeing into the back yard, which was still green despite the fact it was nearly Thanksgiving. Randi watched her go and smiled. Better to give her the false illusion of peace for a while, so the torture would be even more potent later. Oh, no, Randi wasn't loving this...not at all.

Randi wove her way through the throng of laughing, talking morticians and their families. Who knew they were such a lively bunch? She was literally surrounded by short, blonde or red-haired clones. Although, none of them, she smugly noted, was nearly as lovely as Mac.

Randi was in what she considered a crowd of miniatures. Damn, didn't they know inbreeding was dangerous? Wasn't Angus proof enough? She noticed only a few other painfully obvious outsiders. The tall woman felt like the proverbial bastard at a family reunion. *I wonder…if I dressed up like Snow White, would they all follow me home and clean my apartment?*

Then Randi's gaze drifted upward and spotted a shiny, new Volkswagen bug sitting proudly in the parking lot. She groaned out loud and closed her eyes as she pictured the cramped ride home. Shit. It just **had** to be Mac's.

An hour later, Randi was frustrated beyond words that she still hadn't been able to track Mac down. How had 'her' blonde snuck past her? But why should she be surprised? Mac had excelled at stalking…the sneaky runt!

Then she saw her…talking to an elderly couple near the punch bowl. Randi blinked. Mac looked…the older woman searched her mind. *Gorgeous,* her brain belatedly supplied.

The nurse was dressed in tight white jeans and an emerald, satin, long-sleeved blouse. Silver hoop earrings sparkled in the last rays of the day's setting sun when Mac tilted her head toward the sky and let loose a hearty laugh.

Randi stood watching for a moment as the blonde animatedly spoke to the couple. She fought the immediate urge to rush to her side. *GOD!* She frowned. *What is the matter with me? So she looks pretty…and vibrant…and happy. Does that mean we need to be joined at the hip? YES! NO! YES! ARGHHHH!* Randi briefly considered fleeing the party and Mac's life altogether, and her nausea returned.

Mac suddenly stopped talking. As if she sensed Randi's presence, she turned around and looked directly at the darker woman. The tension in Randi's guts immediately eased when Mac's lips shaped into a warm, inviting smile.

Excusing herself from the conversation, Mac deftly moved through the crowd until she was standing in front of Randi. Without hesitation the blonde wrapped her arms around Randi in an affectionate hug. The taller body remained stiff for several seconds, then Randi exhaled shakily and returned the sweet embrace with surprising strength.

"Hey, you. I missed you today," Mac whispered softly in Randi's ear.

Umm... Randi inhaled deeply. *She just washed her hair.* Dark brows knitted together. No one else could have heard what Mac was saying. Mac 'really' missed her?

"I...I...um..." Randi shouldn't have missed her. But she did! As fabulous as it had been tormenting Sandra, a dozen times during the day Randi had considered how much *better* it would have been if Mac were there, too.

Mac pulled back, literally feeling the confusion and tension coursing through Randi's long frame. "It's okay, Randi," she said, making an effort not to sound too disappointed. Mac forced herself to take a step backwards, even though every cell in her body craved closer contact.

Green eyes searched blue, hoping to find even a spark of interest. What she saw was terror mixed with near panic. Mac cursed her foolish hopes and told herself to stop looking for something she'd never see. "Are you ready to put on a good show tonight, partner?"

Randi swallowed audibly. "I...I think so."

"I take it you had a successful day, hero?" Mac motioned with her chin toward the buffet table where Sandra was piling more food on an already overflowing plate.

Randi smiled. She could deal with revenge. "I just happened to mention to Sandra, *in passing*, that it was nice to see she wasn't as skinny as she was in high school." Which was a horrible lie. A stiff wind would blow the bitch all the way to Mexico.

Mac winced but couldn't help the mischievous grin that stretched her face. "How long did she spend in the bathroom after that little comment?"

Randi shrugged and returned the grin. "I got tired of waiting for her."

Both women chuckled, relieving what, to Randi, was a nearly unbearable tension. No. This wasn't *just* tension. It was toe-curling, pulse-racing, wouldn't-it-be-better-if-we-were-rubbing-against-each-other-naked, *sexual* tension! The really good kind.

Randi's eyes widened. This could *not* be happening. She didn't even own any corduroy clothing. She had never been to a WNBA game! A friend had given her free tickets to Lilith Fair, and she had rented a movie instead! Gods above, she had never even seen an episode of 'Xena'! Okay…maybe just a few.

*   *   *

"She's definitely gay," both squirrels said in unison.

"Do you think she was gay before or after she started watching Xena?" the male squirrel asked. "That subtext works like a nasty termite. It undermines the structure of human females from within."

I knew I married him for a reason…other than being knocked-up, that is. "I think it's one of those chicken or egg things," his mate finally offered, sagely.

*   *   *

"Randi, are you okay?" Mac looked worried. What was going on behind those drop-dead gorgeous eyes? Mac stuffed her hands into her pockets, afraid if she touched the older woman right now, Randi would bolt.

"I'm okay," Randi lied. She was nowhere near okay.

Mac took a deep breath of the fragrant night air. Her parents' back yard sloped gently down to the lakefront, and the breeze brought with it the sweet smell of the water. "It doesn't seem like November, does it?" Mac willed the older woman to relax. Being seen together as a couple wouldn't be *that* bad.

Randi shook her head. Everything was messed up, even the weather. It was fall, for Pete's sake. "How were so many people able to come to this 'not a party' on such short notice? We barely made it ourselves."

Mac smiled at Randi's unsubtle movement toward safer ground. "Angus and I were the only ones who really had to travel. The Mackenzies are from Nevada. When my parents moved to Boulder City they were really moving *back* to Boulder City. They both grew up here."

An Aunt walked by and stopped Mac, demanding she be allowed to photograph her lovely niece and beautiful new girlfriend, who, by the way, seemed much nicer than that skanky redhead, Sandra. Randi hesitantly wrapped her arm around Mac, blushing fiercely as the picture was taken and more praise was heaped on Mac for her good taste in lovers. Randi took a deep drink of her wine. Did nothing faze these people?

Mac's sexuality was a non-issue with her family. They greeted Randi without fanfare or rancor. It was obvious that *she* was the only person here who was nervous and worried. No one else cared, with the possible exception of Sandra, the two-timing slut.

Angus approached Sandra at the buffet. "You look nice tonight, Sandra," the doctor offered, trying not to stare at her enormous pile of food on her enormous pile of food.

"What's that supposed to mean?" the redhead hissed. "I can have all the onion dip I want!" With that, Sandra smeared her heaping plate against Angus' chest and stomped off in search of liquor and cake...not in that order.

Angus looked at his shirt helplessly. Were pert tits and not having to be worried about being arrested for solicitation really worth this hassle? Angus smiled. Absolutely! Besides, those damn rechargeable batteries never lasted as long as they advertised. He moved into the house to get a clean shirt.

Sandra spotted Mac and Randi on the way to the cake and made a reluctant detour. "I'm watching you both!" she shrieked. "You can't fool me. This is just some trick."

Randi suddenly grabbed Mac's hand and began pulling her toward the band. "Let's dance."

Green eyes widened. "Uh…okay…but…but, Randi, nobody else is…"

"We're going to dance now…*together*. Is that alright with you, Sandra?" Randi taunted.

Sandra's eyes narrowed, and an evil smile twitched at her lips. *Now* she would catch them at their little game. Randi had *sworn off* dancing in high school. There was no way she'd dance with Mac in front of fifty strangers. "Go ahead then…dance."

AHHHH!!! The bitch had called her bluff. *Of course*, Sandra knew she had sworn off dancing forever! Stupid! Stupid! Stupid!

Mac sensed that Randi was floundering. "C'mon." She took the lead by finding an open spot and wrapping her arms around Randi's neck.

To Randi's dismay, Sandra followed her and Mac every step of the way, grabbing Angus as he stepped out of the patio door. "We're dancing too," she ordered.

"Huh? There's no dancing here!"

"Shut up, Angus, or I won't care how nice your stock portfolio is; it's back to rubber women and whores for you."

Die, Bitch, die! "I'd love to dance, dear."

Mac silently mouthed 'pussy-whipped' to her scowling brother as he and Sandra moved alongside her and Randi, who had yet to start dancing.

"Randi, we need to do something!" Mac whispered. Oh boy, Randi was taking a slow tour of meltdown city.

The taller woman just stared blankly ahead in shock, as Sandra looked on with a satisfied smile.

"Randi?" Mac whispered again, this time placing her lips directly on Randi's ear. "Just relax, hero. I'll lead, if you'll let me." Mac pulled back slightly and grasped one of Randi's dangling hands.

The feeling of Mac's warm palm against hers seized Randi's attention, and she looked down into smiling blue-green eyes. Randi wanted to join Mac in the present, but as Mac began to sway against her in time to the music, Randi was lost in a high school memory.

It was Prom Night and Randi had a date with Rory Johnson, Captain of the football team. The evening had been a raving success until Rory suggested that they actually 'dance' at the dance. He only knew the 'football player shuffle' (where the girl's hands go around the boy's neck, and the boy's hands are wrapped snugly around the girl's waist, and the couple moves in a microscopic circle, in the same spot, and at the same speed, no matter what music is playing). But even 'the shuffle' wasn't **too** terrible until Rory decided it was time to cop a feel.

Randi jumped when two meaty paws grabbed her ass and squeezed it tightly. Then she was blinded by a sudden flurry of flashes. When she stopped seeing spots, she realized Sandra and her gaggle of bitches had preserved the moment for posterity. The photo was blown up to a glorious 8" X 10" and was the only colored picture in a book of all black and white. Randi's humiliation became the inside cover for over six hundred yearbooks. For the Class of '85, it was 'the thing to do' to have "Have a great summer!" written directly over Randi's ass.

*   *   *

"Ahhahahahahahaha!" the male squirrel laughed hysterically. "Ahahahahahahahaha! Whew!" He wiped his eyes with a tiny paw. "That Sandra was a devil!"

Randi narrowed her eyes at the shaking squirrel. Was he laughing at her teenage misery? Grabbing her bag of seeds, she stood and moved over to the animal that was convulsing in the mud.

"It wasn't funny, squirrel," Randi said coldly.

The female squirrel swallowed nervously. Oh well, her mate wanted a murder in the story. She would miss him. She just hoped he didn't have one of those hidden Swiss acorn accounts. They were so hard to access without the proper I.D.

Randi lifted what was easily a half-pound sack of seeds over her head, then simply dropped it.

The male squirrel looked up just in time to see the huge bag of food crash down on his head. His last conscious thoughts were, "In my dreams, there was *always* beer."

The female squirrel shook her head sadly. She knew he would have liked some beer to go along with his last seeds. She could hardly keep him out of those Budweiser cans. Damn, littering college students!

Randi cleared her throat as she sat back down on the bench. "As I was saying…"

*   *   *

Mac's movement was persistent, and Randi found herself unable to ignore the subtle commands of her partner's body, her own body responding without conscious thought. "That's it, hero," Mac encouraged softly as the older woman pulled her closer, and they began to sway in unison.

"Stalker, you're not going to grab my ass, are you?" Randi whispered nervously.

Two eyebrows shot skyward. "I wasn't planning on it, killjoy." Mac made a mental note: No ass grabbing while dancing.

The two couples had broken the ice, and now at least ten other couples were dancing on the soft grass.

Belle and Mac's dad approached Mac and Randi. "Are you girls having a nice time?" Belle asked, wondering whether the girls had had a lovers' quarrel. Randi looked a little shell-shocked.

Mac smiled, certain Randi was having a terrible time. She had to keep reminding herself they were here on a mission, not for fun. "Sure, Mom. By the way, the yard looks beautiful."

Randi nodded in agreement. Soon after the sun disappeared, Chinese lanterns were lit and white Christmas lights that had been strung through the bushes were switched on. The yard was bathed in a soft, twinkling glow. The band even seemed to figure out which ends of their instruments were up, and Randi thought she recognized the tune. The setting was almost...romantic. *Just great,* Randi thought, *like I need more temptation!*

When Mac's parents waltzed away, Randi glanced over at Sandra who was trapped in an endless 'football player shuffle'. Ha! Angus must have been the towel boy. The redhead was staring at Mac with undisguised lust and envy. *That's right, bitch. You lose. I win. Game. Set. Match. Mine!*

Mac looked over at Sandra and Angus, who had somehow drifted closer to her and Randi while dancing. "Sandra, you're letting Angus do the laundry, aren't you?" she queried seriously.

Sandra didn't want to acknowledge Mac's question. *I won't. I won't. I won't.* But in the end, she couldn't help herself. "Why?" she asked warily.

"Well, it's just that your dress is looking a little snug. But I'm sure it's only because he left it in the dryer too long."

Randi looked down at the grass, trying to keep a straight face as Sandra's gaze drifted to the dress that practically swallowed her.

Instantly, blazing brown orbs pinned Angus. Then, without warning, Sandra brought her heel down sharply on his instep. The short doctor began to howl as Sandra moved away from the band, muttering something about chocolate, Tequila, and the bathroom.

Randi and Mac both burst out laughing, and the taller woman suddenly began leading the dance. She dipped Mac gracefully. "You are fantastic," she complimented sincerely.

White teeth and green eyes sparkled brighter than the Christmas lights. "Thanks, Randi!"

Randi spun Mac around and began dancing in earnest. For the next several hours neither woman even checked to see whether Sandra was watching. Instead, they danced and talked and laughed as Mac introduced Randi to the rest of her family.

When her grandfather asked Randi what she did, Mac was ready to intervene and save Randi the embarrassment of saying she was unemployed. But before she could speak, Randi told the elder mortician that she was changing careers, and that she was considering going to college…something she'd always wanted to do. When anxious blue eyes met Mac's, Randi found that Mac was simply beaming.

The last hour was spent in quiet conversation, as though no one else even existed. Finally, Mac tore her eyes away from Randi's long enough to notice that the last of the band members was rolling away a portable keyboard, and the rest of the yard was empty.

"I guess your 'not a party' is over," Randi said softly, not releasing Mac from the casual embrace they'd been in since their last dance.

"I guess." Mac's gaze dropped to the full lips just a few inches in front of her. The blonde's mouth was suddenly dry, and she licked her own lips nervously. Slowly, she brought her right hand up to rest beneath silky black tresses and on top of the soft, fine hairs at the nape of Randi's neck. She wouldn't get another chance like this and she knew it. She wanted this so badly, her soul fairly ached for it! Mac felt as though she would die if she didn't kiss Randi this very moment.

Randi's pulse began to quicken, and she suddenly became very aware of the warm body in her arms. Mac's satin blouse felt cool against her hot fingertips, and she was vaguely aware that she was drowning in the dilated pools of emerald so close to her.

Mac leaned forward until the entire length of her body was pressed firmly against Randi. A gust of warm wind blew dark strands of hair over the taller woman's shoulders, causing them to gently tickle Mac's neck.

Mac gasped when Randi's hands slid around the small of her back, pulling her closer still. Mac knew she should stop. This wasn't what Randi wanted. She'd made that abundantly clear. But none of that mattered to Mac at this very second. The blonde slowly brought herself up on tiptoe, drawing a soft moan from Randi when her taut nipples brushed against the taller woman's.

When Mac's lips were only a hairbreadth away, Randi whispered softly, "There's no one watching us."

Mac pulled away ever so slightly. "Does it really matter?" she breathed, praying it didn't.

Randi didn't answer. Instead, she closed her eyes and ducked her head until she felt Mac's gentle breath caress her lips and the hand on her neck tighten its grip. Another heartbeat and the softest, feather-light touch she'd ever felt brushed against her…

"Morag!!" Angus shouted from the back porch, startling both women.

Randi instantly pulled back, confused eyes darting wildly around the empty yard. "I…I…God, I…didn't," Randi stuttered as her heartbeat thundered in her ears.

"Dad needs you to move your car RIGHT NOW! Uncle Albert's blocked in by that ugly piece of shit you bought. He's been wanting to leave for the last hour, and he's tired of waiting!" Angus yelled.

Mac ignored her brother and took a step towards Randi, who was backing away from her with her hands held up as if to forestall Mac's advance. Shit! Mac's stomach clenched when she saw the look of sheer panic in Randi's eyes. "Randi, wait!" she called after the older woman who suddenly turned and began running toward the lake. "No! Wait!"

Mac moved to follow her but was interrupted by her father's insistent voice. "Morag, get up here and move that car! You can kiss your woman later."

Mac hesitated for just a second, then watched ruefully as Randi disappeared into the night. Randi's rejection stung just like she knew it would. No, that was a lie. It more than stung. What the hell was she thinking? Randi could never have *real* feelings for her. The darker woman came right out and told her it would be *impossible* to love her that very first night when they agreed to this wretched plan. Mac's heart twisted painfully in her chest. But it had felt so real! Tears stung her eyes as she sped up her pace into the house. "Tell Uncle Albert to give me a second...I just need to get my bag."

*　*　*

Randi's feet hung over the edge of the dock, dangling in the warm water. The moonlight reflected off the lake, giving the entire area an almost ethereal quality. The entire evening had been like that.

Things with Mac and her family hadn't gone as planned. The tall woman laughed cruelly. Big shock. Why should this night be any different from the rest of her life? Nothing ever went as planned.

She wasn't supposed to start having feelings for Mac or start liking Mac's parents. She tried to continue to deny it, but couldn't. Randi *liked* it when Mac touched her. She *wanted* Mac to touch her. She craved it. Mac's skin was soft and warm, and when the nurse held her hand, the grip was firm and comforting. When Randi looked into those sea-green eyes she felt...something more than friendship.

Randi recognized the first familiar signs of panic and let them come. What was she doing?! How did things get so out of control? She hated out of control. She was going to kiss Mac...not for show, not for Sandra, but for herself! Christ, if Angus hadn't broken her out of her spell, she would have crawled underneath the woman's skin in an attempt to get closer!

Being around Mac was like peering over the edge of a cliff. It was frightening and exhilarating and somehow, no matter how close Randi got to the edge, she still found herself inching forward, despite herself. It was as though some unknown force had grabbed her by the collar and was threatening to send her free falling. She felt like she was fighting gravity itself. The confusing part was, Randi didn't know why she was fighting at all.

Randi desperately wanted some pain tablets for her throbbing head, but decided they probably wouldn't mix well with all the strawberry wine she'd consumed. *I need to go apologize to Mac. I shouldn't have run away like that. She probably thinks…Hell, who am I kidding? I have no clue what she thinks. Although, I'm quite certain the words 'asshole' and 'tease' will be mixed in there somewhere.*

"Randi?"

"Yes?" Randi turned her head and wiped her eyes as Belle sat down next to her on the dock.

"Morag asked me to give you this." Belle held out a slender wooden box with a note attached. Randi's eyes widened. She knew that box! She'd seen it displayed at the mathematics competition! Her hands shook as she reverently grasped the cool, wooden container. Then her heart stopped beating.

"Why…" Randi swallowed past the sudden lump in her throat. "Why isn't Mac giving me this herself?"

Belle sighed. Morag was always so brave in everything *except* matters of the heart. What had she gone and done this time? "I don't know, child. Morag tore out of here in that awful little car of hers." Randi immediately closed her eyes, and Belle's heart went out to the young brunette. Sometimes love just sucked.

The tiny woman rose to her feet and clasped Randi's shoulder firmly. "She took her bags with her and said goodbye to me. I don't think she's coming back."

"I see." Randi gazed out at the still lake, feeling sick.

"Have faith, Randi," Belle said quietly as she left the younger woman to her thoughts.

Several long moments later, with shaking hands, Randi opened the note, which was easily readable in the bright moonlight.

Hero,

I shouldn't have tried to kiss you. I'm sorry. I just couldn't help myself. I fully admit that I'm taking the coward's way out by leaving without talking to you. I'm a coward. I'm sorry about that, too.

There'll be a plane ticket waiting for you at the Northwest ticket counter. I'm sure Mom will drive you.

I believe this belongs to you. Wear it in good health, Randi. You deserve it.

Despite everything, I'll always think of this as a great trip. We really did make a wonderful team.

Love,
Mac

Randi ran the tip of her finger along the faint script, lingering over the last two words. *Love, Mac.* She folded the note closed. *Love? Love.*

Randi laid the note aside and carefully lifted the wooden box that weighed almost nothing. She'd gotten everything she came for. Sandra was probably *still* in the bathroom. And in her hands was the prize she'd been seeking for 15 years. *So why do I feel like what I should really be after is driving across the desert without me?*

Randi pushed herself to her feet, and she looked down at the small box once more before launching it forward with all her might. She watched it for just a second or two before it disappeared, and she heard a tiny, far off splash.

It was time to go home.

CHAPTER 9

The male squirrel weakly poked his fuzzy head out from under the heavy bag of seeds. A groan escaped his lips, assuming squirrels have lips, and he shook his tiny head, trying to dispel the loud ringing in his ears. What was that? He focused on the faint, ragged sounds coming from the bench. Crying? Yes! His heartbroken mate was weeping over his untimely demise! He knew he made the right choice when he married the somewhat promiscuous but highly desirable female squirrel. *Mama don't know squat!*

And look at the teary-eyed human. Don't worry, human! It's not a crime to be clumsy!

The female squirrel was sitting on the bench next to Randi, shaking uncontrollably. "Boohoohoohoo," she sobbed. "Boohoohoohoo." She *knew* if she was patient "The Story of Me" would turn out to be a tragic love story!

Randi glanced over at the male squirrel. "Joining us again, I see." Whew! The tall woman didn't need homicide…err…rodentcide…on her already burdensome conscience.

The female squirrel followed Randi's gaze. Her mate was alive! She jumped down off the bench and watched proudly as he struggled free of the lethal sack of seeds. How could she have given up on him so easily? Shame colored her cheeks, though oddly, they still appeared brown.

Wasn't it her mate who, just last spring, had thrown himself in front of an oncoming lawnmower in order to save her life?

"Don't fret, Sweetheart. It takes more than a human to do me in!" He smiled at the admiration that shone clearly in her eyes. Ever since he dove in front of that lawnmower to rescue that half-full beer can, he'd been livin' on easy street! He shifted his attention to the very sad looking human, then back to his mate.

"What did I miss? What did I miss?" he asked eagerly.

"Umm...Nothing. You'll catch on." *Not!*

The rain had stopped, and the sky was now filled with a million bright stars. Randi stood up and shook her soaked jacket, scattering icy water droplets in all directions. Deep blue eyes naturally drifted to the small apartment building. There was only one apartment with its light left on. Somehow she knew it was Mac's.

"I've been back in town for nearly five days now." Randi sniffed and rolled her stiff shoulders. "Mac's back, too. I went over to the hospital today to stalk my stalker." The woman cocked her head as if to really consider the question; "Life is really twisted sometimes, isn't it?"

The squirrels had no choice but to agree. In the wild, untamed world of the City Park, they'd damned near seen it all.

Randi took a deep breath and gathered her courage. "Enjoy the seeds, rats. It's about time I got an ending to my story." And with that, the human began walking toward the apartment complex.

The male squirrel looked at his mate in horror. "I'll catch on, huh? Not! She's leaving!"

"No!!!!!!" both the squirrels shouted in concert. What did she mean 'get' an ending? There was no ending now?! ARGGGHHHHH! Didn't the human know how long these past few hours had been in squirrel years?

The female squirrel stomped her paw dramatically. "I gave her the best damn years of my life!"

Oh, the misery! The male squirrel starting crying pathetically.

"It'll be okay," his mate comforted softly, grabbing hold of her own tenuous emotions. "I've got an idea." Her beady, black eyes took on a determined glint. "We'll know what happens to the human woman…or *you'll* die trying!" she declared.

The male squirrel paled, although strangely, he too still just looked brown. "Uh Oh."

*   *   *

Randi stood outside the apartment complex door with both hands in her pockets. Maybe it was a security building, and she wouldn't be able to get in? She could always go the hospital and find Mac tomorrow. Randi tested the doorknob, sighing when it turned easily. Maybe not.

The lobby wasn't just warm—it was hot. And the drastic change in temperature caused the woman to shiver violently. She immediately peeled off wet gloves and held her hands over the radiator. *God, I'm colder than a witch's tit,* she mused as she sniffed for the hundredth time in the last five minutes.

The unemployed driving instructor scanned the resident listings and a building map. *Mackenzie 201.* Mac's apartment was on the corner of the second floor facing the park. *I knew that was her light. She's still awake. Crap, no more excuses.*

The tall woman tried to calm her nerves and order her scattered thoughts. They were a jumble of conflicting emotions and feelings. And Randi hated feelings. Not *all* feelings, just the Debby Boone version and messy, pathetic feelings. Like fear.

Fear was one *very* big, *very* compelling feeling. Fear, with a little help from Sandra, the lying trollop, had turned a mathematical genius into a second rate driving instructor. What had already colored Randi's past, threatened to steal her future.

Randi stopped outside the door with a gold number 201. She closed her eyes. This was her last chance to stop before she made a colossal fool of herself. Not that that had been much of a deterrent before in her life, but still…

Dark eyebrows drew together in deep concentration. Was love more compelling than fear? Nope. It was ultimately fear that had brought her to this point—and she knew it. One fear was just stronger than the other. Randi was simply afraid *not* to try to capture what she had only caught the barest glimpse of in the car on the way to Nevada, and in an empty corn field along the side of the road, and in a small stinky jail cell, and most definitely in the Mackenzie's back yard.

Her mind's eye flashed to a moonlit dock and a neatly written note whose simple words had rocked her to the core. *Love.* Did Mac mean it? Was that what this was?

Face it, fool. You went and fell in love with your stalker. Randi let out a shaky breath and felt the healing power of acceptance. Just saying the words in her mind released a pressure that had been building almost from the very beginning. But that stark truth brought with it a whole new set of fears. Chiefly, what if Mac wouldn't accept her love? A band tightened around Randi's chest, and she gasped at the intensity of its strength.

I'll just keep trying until she gives me a chance! The pang deep in her heart eased even as her stomach threatened to rebel. *Or else, I'll get really scared and freak out and throw up all over her. One of the two.*

Randi shook her head to clear it. Enough with the guessing and mushy, philosophical bullshit! She had ass to kiss and a girl to convince. White teeth flashed in an almost feral smile. *Ready or not, stalker, here I come.*

Randi lifted her hand to knock on the door, but before she could strike the wood the door opened.

"Thanks, Mac. I'll see you later," an attractive blonde called over her shoulder as the bedroom door slammed. She took a step, without turning her head, and ran smack dab into Randi. "Oh, excuse me." She pointedly looked around the tall woman who was clearly blocking her path.

The former driving instructor didn't say a word out loud. Internally, however, several extremely loud voices were raging. The main theme went something like, *"She's got a fuckin' girlfriend already?! Jesus Christ, she's been home less than two days!"*

The blonde's eyes widened as she took in the soaking wet woman in front of her. This was a friend of Mac's? "Mac's in the bedroom, I was just leaving."

"You sure as hell were! Here, let me help you!" Randi grabbed the front of the woman's denim shirt and pulled her into the hall. "And don't come back!" she shouted as she made her way into the apartment without so much as a backward glance. It wasn't easy to look intimidating with snot running out of her nose…but Randi managed to do a fairly decent job.

"Sheesh, I was already going," the woman complained, trying not to stumble. "How rude!" she murmured as she made her way down the hall. Oh well, the tall brunette was already nicer than that skinny slut Sandra.

Randi shut the door behind her just as Mac emerged from the bedroom wearing only a powder-blue bra and French cut panties.

The older woman tried not to stare at the feminine but muscular form in front of her, although she sincerely appreciated the rush of hot blood toward her extremities…and other vital body parts.

"Randi?!" Mac jumped when she suddenly saw the woman standing in her living room. "You scared the crap out of me!"

"Who the hell was she?" Randi folded her arms in front her chest.

"What?" Mac went scurrying for something to cover herself. She'd spent the last six days in misery over the way she left things with

Randi. The last thing she needed was to be standing in her underwear, facing the woman she had told herself was off limits. "What are you doing here?"

"Answer my question first," Randi said in harsh, flat voice.

Randi's tone stopped Mac dead in her tracks and the blonde felt her hackles rise. "What business is it of yours?" she said slowly through clenched teeth.

*   *   *

"Tell me what you see! Hurry up!" the male squirrel hissed.

"Shut up!" The female squirrel thumped him on the head, drawing a loud grunt. "It's not easy to listen through the glass you know." She stood on her mate's shoulders as she peered into Mac's second story window.

The male squirrel was perched on a rickety piece of vine that clung to the building but unfortunately changed directions about a foot and a half below the window. He groaned under his mate's weight. Damn rotten, gangster-ridden construction unions and their greedy-ass kickbacks. What kind of builder is too cheap for a window ledge?

"Hold still," the female complained.

"What do you see?! Tell me now, or I'm sending us both careening to our deaths!"

"Fine," she groused, unhappy at the interruption. "The tall human yanked some blonde out the front door and then walked into the apartment."

"Morag?"

"Ha! You finally figured out who she was. Good for you!"

"Well...?" he asked impatiently. "You're not getting any lighter, you know. Humph!" Another paw to the head was meant to improve his attitude. No more cheese-coated popcorn for his mate. She was friggin' huge!

"No, it was some other woman. I don't think she's important to the story. Oooooh, this must be Mac." She watched as a petite, fair-haired human moved into the living room with Randi. "She's nearly naked!"

"Ewww!!!" The male squirrel was suddenly grateful for his position on the bottom. That guy in the long trenchcoat had given him all the taste of naked human he ever wanted, thank you very much.

"Mac's hands are on her hips. Now she's shaking a finger at the tall human."

"A fight?" Was the storyteller completely hopeless? "Has she even *tried* to remove Mac's fleas?"

"I don't think so," the female purred as her eyes glazed over with lust. *Ohh, he's so got my number.*

"Wasn't Mac naked the first time she went to the other human's apartment?"

"No, it was the other way around. Do you think it's some sort of human ritual?"

The male shrugged, causing his mate to wobble dangerously.

"HOLD STILL!!!"

"Sorry."

"Ohhh, I think the fight's over. Mac hands aren't flailing around anymore, and the taller human is staring at her shoes."

"She lost."

"Yep."

*　　*　　*

"I didn't see any Tupperware in her hand," Randi offered sheepishly.

"That's because she was *returning* it. For God's sake, what's wrong with you?"

"It's really late."

"It's 11 o'clock, and she said she saw my light on."

"But you're almost naked!" the former driving instructor groaned.

"How perceptive. I thought I was alone, and I was on my way to the shower. Is that all right with you, Randi?" Mac added sarcastically.

Randi nodded and stepped forward out of the shadow she had backed into during Mac's tirade. God, but the woman had a bad temper!

Mac gasped. "You're all wet!"

"I…I…"

The blonde grabbed a box of tissues from the end table on the way to the older woman. She yanked out a wad of tissue and held it to Randi's nose. "Blow."

"But…"

"I said blow!"

Randi immediately complied, wondering if the nurse had been a drill sergeant or mother in a former life. "Thanks."

Mac tossed the tissue into the wastebasket, then reached up and stroked Randi's wind-burned cheeks with the back of her hand. Mac's hand moved upward, and she pushed aside the damp bangs stuck to Randi's forehead, flattening her palm to feel moist, hot skin.

The darker woman leaned into the cool touch.

Pale brows furrowed with worry. "You have a fever."

Randi's eyes swept down Mac's body. *You're lucky I haven't had a heart attack.* "I'm feeling fine."

"Shut up. Tell me why you're here."

Randi's eyes widened as she tried to figure out how to comply with Mac's request. Finally, she just gave up. "Huh?"

* * *

As soon as the female squirrel relayed the words, her mate began to howl with laughter. "The tall human is the guy! I knew it!"

The female squirrel just groaned.

*   *   *

Mac blushed when she realized what she'd said. "I mean…Don't shut up, and please tell me what you're doing here."

Randi tried to maintain eye contact. She really did. But it was impossible. The woman wasn't wearing any clothes! And she was gorgeous!

Green eyes rolled. "Just a minute." Mac disappeared into the bedroom, then returned wearing a soft, knee-length robe.

Randi looked at the now respectably-clad woman. Relief was warring with disappointment and losing…badly.

"Talk," Mac commanded as she stripped off Randi's soaked coat. It weighed a ton. Mac scowled. Why was the crazy woman out in the freezing rain?

"I…um…I wanted to apologize."

"What for?" the blonde asked as she began unbuttoning Randi's shirt.

"For running away instead of talking to you."

Mac just nodded.

"What um…what are you doing?"

"You're freezing. You need a hot shower," she answered, as though that explained the fact that she was undressing the woman. Then Mac stopped and looked at her hands as though they had a mind of their own. "I'm sorry. I…"

Randi grabbed the suddenly shaky hands. "Don't be sorry." She swallowed hard. This was the important part. "I'm not."

Mac suddenly looked up. "But you said…"

"Forget what I said. I was an idiot…a scared-out-of-her-wits idiot."

Mac laid her palms flat against Randi's chest. She could feel the older woman's heart pounding wildly. Could she mean…? "Are you saying you're 'interested' in me?" Mac was tempted to wriggle her eyebrows for effect but managed to resist the impulse.

"Yes."

"No."

"What?"

"I said no." Mac suddenly backed away as if she were afraid to stand too close to Randi.

"You're turning me down?" *NO!!! SHOT DOWN! CRASH AND BURN!! REJECTION!!*

"Yes."

Mac's words were unequivocal, but there was a slight hesitation in her voice, and Randi pounced. "Why?"

"Because, hero, I'm not an experiment. What was impossible before, is now possible? You don't know what, much less who, you want."

Randi stepped forward and wrapped her arms around Mac's waist. "That's not true," she said softly. "I do know."

Tears immediately sprang into Mac's eyes as she weakly tried to pull away. "It is true," she persisted, her resolve already waning.

"It's not. I promise." Randi tightened her hold and pulled Mac closer.

Mac shook her head 'no', so Randi continued. "I was confused and scared. And to tell the truth, I'm still scared…just not *so* confused."

Randi brought up one hand and gently cupped Mac's chin, forcing eye contact. She waited until glistening green locked on blue. "Mac…"

The smaller woman nearly swooned at the sound of her name. It was the first time Randi had called her anything other than 'stalker'. Although she had to admit, the nickname was starting to grow on her.

"I'm sure that I want you."

"Randi…" Mac wiped her eyes with the back of her hand. "You have to be sure. I just couldn't take it if you just up and decided that…"

Mac's words were cut off when two fingers were gently pressed against her mouth. "I promise," Randi said as she slowly moved forward to claim the soft lips she didn't want to live without.

Mac closed her eyes and tossed her fears to the wind, rolling the dice with her heart one more time. Some things were worth the risk. A split second before their mouths touched, when she could feel Randi's breath mix with her own, the older woman stopped.

"I should tell you, Mac. I think I'm getting sick," Randi whispered.

"Like I care," Mac breathed as she surged forward and crossed the tiny distance between them.

The lips brushed together gently, then with more pressure. The kiss wasn't the least bit tentative, but it was achingly soft, and sweet, and exceeded Randi's expectations in the first few seconds alone. Randi couldn't stop the moan that escaped her throat at the delicious touch.

Mac firmly told herself to go slowly, but when the lips brushing hers parted ever so slightly, she couldn't help but deepen the kiss. Hot tongues collided, and there was another moan, this time Mac's. Small hands tangled in dark, wet hair, and both women threw themselves into the kiss as though it might be their very last. Pulses raced as hands and mouths sought closer contact still.

Finally, Randi pulled back gasping for air. Damn! Now *that* was what a kiss was supposed to be like.

Mac's body was on fire. She drew her fingertips across Randi's lips in simple awe. Wow! More than wow. Then nervously she looked up to meet deep blue eyes. "Are you okay, hero?" *Oh God, she'd better be, or I'm going to die right here.*

The younger woman was immediately pulled into a fierce embrace. Randi nodded her head as a sudden surge of emotion closed her throat and caused tears to sting her eyes. "Yeah," her voice cracked a little as she spoke. "I'm great."

Mac smiled into the soft skin of Randi's throat, then kissed it gently before pulling away. She held out her hand. "Shower?"

Randi took the younger woman's hand and intertwined their fingers as they slowly moved toward the bathroom. "Alone?"

"Pretty sure of yourself. Huh, beautiful? What if I'm not that kind of girl?" Mac smiled impishly. Okay, it was a stretch, but Randi didn't need to know that.

"What if *I* am?!" Randi smirked. "Besides, I've already met your parents. Don't tell me there's *more* that I have to do to properly court you. I've already taken you to the best jail in the south, and that's not enough?"

Mac cocked her head to the side and scrunched up her nose speculatively. "Could be."

"You want to hear the 'L' word, doncha? I knew it." Randi pulled open the bathroom door. "Fine. I'll be the first one to say it. *Lucky.* I *really* want to get *lucky.*"

Mac laughed and shook her head. "Sorry, hero. Try again," she teased as she pulled two aqua-colored towels out of the hall closet.

"'Loofah'? You've got a big old loofah sponge in there, and you're going to scrub my back?"

Mac giggled as she walked into the bathroom ahead of Randi.

"I've got it! 'Lozenge'. I could sooo use a throat lozenge."

Mac's robe landed on the floor at Randi's feet. Blue eyes widened, and Randi hummed appreciatively. "Tease! Oohhh, 'luscious'. Luscious is such a good 'L' word."

A bra sailed right over Randi's head, and the taller woman's jaw dropped. "Lord, have mercy," she croaked. "Okay, the word is *lust.* I'm certain."

An enormous grin shaped Randi's lips when a naked arm suddenly reached out of the bathroom and tugged her inside.

* * *

The female squirrel let out a deep, contented sigh. She loved happy endings.

"Well, what was the 'L' word?!" her mate asked. "I'll bet it was lice. The blonde human was hinting about grooming. I tried to tell Randi!"

The female rolled her eyes. "Let's go home," she said as she dropped gracefully from her mate's shoulders to the rain-soaked vine alongside him.

* * *

"OH MY GOD!" came Randi's cry, loud enough for the squirrels to hear her on the way down the building.

* * *

"I guess she finally figured it out," the male speculated as he jumped onto the sidewalk. Way to go, human!

"It looks like the female human wasn't so dumb after all."

"Nope." He sighed happily when his paws left the hard concrete and dug into rich moist soil. "Even a human will eventually figure things out when it's true *luuuuvvvvv.*"

The female's smile was broad enough to show her sharp pointy canines and stretch her furry squirrel face.

"Ohhh…Look! The serial killer is back, and he brought Ritz Crackers! Let's go!"

The couple took off across the park, trailing the small, intellectual-looking young man with the shovel. The rodents plopped down in front of their bench and snuggled together to fend off the cold night air. The female couldn't help but look back. Her gaze drifted upward just in time to see Mac's curtains being drawn and the small apartment go black.

The man settled into his story. "I wasn't an easy child to potty train…."

The End. Almost.

Disclaimer: No squirrels were harmed during the production of this story. Although priests, morticians, sluts, proctologists, Big Gulps, Debby Boone, Scottish names, Bill and Hillary Clinton, Volkswagens, 'that ugly chick', gym teachers, eating disorders, Dr. Pepper, and stalkers were all seriously maligned.

What ever happened to? (In no particular order)

Paula's (Randi's sister) kids—got a book deal for their story, which is tentatively entitled "Auntie Dearest". You can find it under the 'whiny loser relatives who leech off someone with their own life' section at amazon.com. Order in time for the holidays.

Angus—finally got fed up with Sandra. Taking his cue from Mac, he fled into the night after the 'not a party'. Opting for the peace of the open road, Angus rented a Mercedes and began driving. On the way home, he was stopped for speeding by a police officer named Bubba. Angus served 30 days in jail for resisting arrest and used that time to get in touch with his 'feminine side'.

The male squirrel—became a raging alcoholic, but was ultimately redeemed, becoming president of The Potter Park A.S.S. (Alcoholic Squirrel Society). He is truly an inspiration to his fellow rodent.

Bubba—is thoroughly enjoying Angus' feminine side. Upon Angus' release from jail, he and Angus opened a gourmet pet food shop. They are expecting their first child in November.

Belle—received a computer for Christmas. She began reading, then writing, 'Star Trek' fan fiction. She was assimilated. Mac's father has planned an intervention for "once the busy dyin' season is over".

The jailer—who the hell cares about the jailer?

Sandra—has been on the run ever since it was discovered that the one wall of her locker room office was a two-way mirror. She is now a fugitive from justice and was featured on last month's 'America's Most Wanted'. If seen, do not approach. She is believed to be armed and dangerous and hiding somewhere in the state of Texas (where someone keeps scratching off the weight listed on her wanted poster so that it reads 97 pounds. She was listed as 98).

Mac's father—is still doing what he loves. Whenever he walks by, people always say, "Nobody loves dead people like Mac!"

The priest that Randi screwed during the Christmas Eve church service in 1993—was transferred to Australia, where he was cast in a remake of 'The Thorn Birds'. God, he loves 'method acting'!

The female squirrel—finally listened to her mother and left her mate. After a brief 'wild period' where she was courted by small skunks, she came to her senses and tried to reclaim her squirrel soulmate. They are currently in couples' therapy.

Cletus—was actually named Bill Gates by his adopted parents. He is evil incarnate.

Randi and Mac—do you even have to ask? They, of course, lived happily ever after.

Cast of Characters (Okay, this is a book, NOT a movie. But if it WERE a movie, and I WERE the casting director, which I WOULD BE because in my fantasy realm I RULE THE UNIVERSE, these are the folks that would get the casting nod):

Randi: Dar

Mac/Morag: Renee O'Connor (I can't find that funky little accent for the 'wrong' letter of her first name...but you know who I mean)

Sandra: Jennifer Aniston

Angus: Ted Raimi

Belle: Cheryl Ladd

Mac's Dad: Bond, James Bond

Bubba: the President of the United States of America, Mr. Bill Clinton

The priest that Randi screwed during the Christmas Eve church service in 1993: Tom Selleck

The male squirrel: Alf

The female squirrel: Chip, but sometimes Dale

The Actual End.